Her heart was beating like mad.

His hands, firm and strong, caught her shoulders, and he was so close that she felt his breath in her hair. He smelled of spice and tobacco, and the muscular warmth of his body enveloped her from head to toe. She couldn't quite breathe, and she didn't dare look up.

"You've avoided looking at me all morning," he said quietly. "Is it because I tried to kiss you...or because I stopped too soon?"

Her face burned in reaction. And still she couldn't look up. Her lips parted on a rush of breath. She lifted her face then, and her misty green eyes sought his. He seemed to stop breathing and just stared at her. He didn't smile. His eyes searched, probed.

"Don't be afraid of me, Kit," he said, his voice deep and slow and soft.

"You're a stranger...."

He shook his head. "No. You're just looking at me in a different way."

"Nobody tops Diana Palmer when it comes to delivering pure, undiluted romance."
—Jayne Ann Krentz

DIANA PALMER

Champagne Girl

MIRA BOOKS

RECYCLED PAPER · RECYCLED PAPER

MIRA

ISBN 1-55166-292-2

CHAMPAGNE GIRL

Printed in U.S.A.

For Melinda, Aurora and Pat of Texas

Chapter One

Comanche Flats was one of the biggest ranches around, and Catherine Blake always felt a sense of small-town friendliness in the town that had grown up around the ranch. Friendliness and peace. Not that Matt gave her much peace, but she did enjoy the company of her mother and her other stepcousins.

She grinned as she wheeled her small rebuilt white Volkswagen convertible between neat white fences to the big Spanish stucco house beyond, her pale-green eyes on the distant line of oaks visible across the prairie. There were twenty-two square miles of land on this ranch, an hour or so out of Fort Worth,

Texas, that her great-uncle had built into an empire. It was always described as lying between the Eastern and Western Cross Timbers, long bands of oaks, once formidable, but now reduced in numbers by encroaching civilization. The bands ran from north to south, and in the days of the great cattle drives they had been a point of reference for cattlemen.

Her slender hand brushed back her dark-chestnut hair from her oval, olive-complexioned face, and she felt again a wild thrill of excitement at having graduated from college with a degree in journalism. While at college in Fort Worth, she'd lived in a dorm during the week and come home on weekends. Often Matt had flown over to get her. The ranch was far enough away from the sprawling Dallas-Fort Worth airport that Matt preferred flying in his private plane, which had a hangar at the tiny airport in Comanche Flats. Catherine smiled, thinking about that, proud of her graduation with honors and her promise of a good job in New York. Matthew Dane Kincaid might pull everybody else's strings, but he was through pulling Catherine's as of now. She was almost twenty-two and feeling feverish with independence.

She was just returning from a four-day trip to San Antonio, where she'd tried to find work at a small public relations firm. That hadn't panned out, but through a contact she'd obtained a job at a bigger firm in New York. The job wasn't open immediately; it would take several weeks for her office to be readied. But she must have impressed the executive vice-president, because he'd flown all the way down to San Antonio to check out her credentials and had hired her on the spot. She felt excited about that. And about having the opportunity to escape her family. And, especially, Matt.

Odd, she thought, how possessive he'd gotten since her graduation from college. He owned the ranch where she and her mother lived, of course, and the feedlot, and he even had a controlling interest in the local real estate companies. But he was only a stepcousin, and Catherine deeply resented his domination. The loss of her father—he had died during the Vietnam War, when she was a baby—had made her independent-minded at an early age,

and she'd fought Matt tooth and nail for years
for every inch of freedom she had. When she
wasn't dying of unrequited love for him, she
admitted bitterly. Hal and Jerry were never so
overbearing. Of course, Matt's brothers lacked
his fiery temper and shrewd business mind.
And his inborn arrogance. Matt made arrogance an art.

Betty Blake, all silvery hair and bright eyes
and laughter, came rushing down the steps to
meet her daughter.

"Darling, you're home!" she enthused.
"How lovely to have you back!"

"It was only for four days," Catherine reminded her as she returned her mother's hug.
"How did Matt take it?"

"He's barely spoken to me," Betty confessed. "Oh, Kit, you've landed me in the fire
this time!"

"I have to be independent," Catherine said,
her green eyes wide and pleading. "Matt just
wants his own way again, as usual, but this
time he isn't winning. I'll go if I have to wait
on tables. But I won't need to," she said stub-
bornly. "I still have my income from the
stock. I'll live on that!"

Betty started to speak but nibbled on her lower lip instead. "Come in and get settled," she said eventually. "Did you get the job?"

"Not the one in San Antonio," Catherine said with a sigh. She glowered. "Imagine, having to sneak off and make up stories about holidays with a nonexistent girlfriend just to go and apply! Honestly, Matt is such a tyrant...." She grinned at her mother's worried face. "I won't start again, I promise. Anyway, I did get a job. But it's in New York."

"New York!" Betty looked shocked.

"It pays well, and I don't start for a month. Plenty of time to get ready."

"Matt won't like it," Betty said grimly.

"Matt doesn't matter!"

"You know better than that," Betty replied. "Without Matt, you and I would be living in low-income housing right now. You know your father got us up to our ears in debt just before he was killed in Vietnam. I've told you often enough."

"And Great-Uncle Henry got us out of trouble and brought us to live with him. Yes, I know," she said broodingly. She followed her mother into the enormous house where the beauty of the Spanish styling of the hall and staircase staggered her as much now as it had in her childhood. Betty had been raised in this house, too, by Uncle Henry. "Oh, I love this house," Catherine murmured.

"Your great-uncle was quite a man," Betty said with a laugh. "He had style and taste."

"Except in wives," Catherine muttered darkly.

"Just because Matt's mother was young is no excuse for a remark like that. You know very well she adored Henry. And she gave him three strong step-sons, too."

Catherine didn't reply. She and her mother went up the winding staircase leading to Catherine's bedroom. Matt and Hal, who were both bachelors, lived at the other side of the enormous, sprawling house. Jerry and his wife, Barrie, lived in a house farther down the ranch road.

"The family are all coming for dinner tomorrow night," Betty remarked. "Matt flew to Houston this afternoon, but he'll be back late tonight, I expect. The rains have been horrible. We're expecting more tonight, and there are flash-flood warnings out. I do hope he'll fly carefully.''

"At least he's not driving, thank God. Matt has never driven carefully,'' Catherine said dryly. "How many cars did he wreck before he got out of college?''

Betty laughed. "Not as many as Hal did.''

Catherine stopped on the way down the hall to stare at the huge portrait of Great-Uncle Henry that hung on the wall between a pair of sconces. "I don't like him up here,'' she said as she studied the face that was so much like her late grandfather's—dark hair and green eyes and an olive complexion, the features Catherine had inherited from her mother's people. "He belongs downstairs in the living room,'' she added absently.

"I can't watch television with him glaring at me,'' Betty said reasonably. "Besides, I always feel safe going down the hall in the dark, knowing he's here.''

Catherine laughed softly. "Oh, Mama.''

"He was my idol when I was growing up.'' The older woman smiled, staring at the portrait. "I adored him. I still do.''

"Even though he provided you with a step-aunt half your age?"

"I like Evelyn quite well, in fact," Betty answered softly. "She took great care of all of us. My parents died when I was so young; I barely remember them." She sighed. "I miss your father so much sometimes...."

"So do I, Mama." Catherine hugged her gently and gave her a sound kiss on the cheek. "I'm glad I've got you," she said warmly, then quickly changed the subject. "Now, come and tell me all the news! I'm terribly out of touch."

Betty and Catherine sat down to dinner alone, listening to Annie's mutterings as she waddled around the table putting food on it.

"Never can get the family together all at one time," Annie grumbled, glaring at the food as if it were responsible for her dilemma. "Mr. Hal never shows up until Mr. Matt yells at him, and Mr. Jerry and Miss Barrie gone off again, and—"

"We'll eat twice as much," Catherine promised the buxom, white-haired woman who'd come there with Matt's mother.

Annie relented. "Well, I made enough. We can freeze some, I guess."

She went back into the kitchen, and Catherine and Betty exchanged knowing glances.

"Where is Hal, anyway?" Catherine asked.

"I don't know. Before Matt left, he told him to help the boys move some cattle off the flats, and Hal went out into the rain in a huff. He hates getting wet, you know."

"He hates taking orders more," the younger woman replied.

"A trait he shares with you, my darling." Betty sighed as she lifted her fork. "I do hope you won't start right in on Matt. He's been in a terrible temper since you left."

"I'll wait a day or two, all right?"

Betty looked faintly apprehensive. "All right."

Catherine had gone to bed when Hal came in. She heard him talking to Betty as he went past her door. Good old Hal, she thought with a smile. He was her only ally in Matt's family. She and Hal were a lot alike, both renegades, both refugees from Matt's authority.

She closed her eyes and slept, feeling safe

and comfortable in her warm bed, hearing the rain come down in torrents. She wondered if Matt would be able to fly back tonight.

A few hours later the sound of a motor awakened her, and she lifted the window curtain beside the bed to peek out. The outside lights were ablaze, and a tall, lean man in a distinctive tan trench coat and a silverbelly Stetson was getting out of a car. He lifted an attaché case and plowed toward the house in the drenching rain. Matt!

With faint misgivings she stared down at his hard, formidable face. It was a shock to catch Matt unawares; he was almost always light-hearted and smiling when he was around Catherine. He smiled more with her than with anyone else. But when he didn't know she was looking, he became a stranger. Matt was a puzzle she'd never solved. Most of his men were afraid of him, although he was never unfair or overly demanding. It was that air of authority he wore, the remnants of his strict upbringing.

Matt was the oldest of Evelyn's sons from her first marriage, and from all accounts, his childhood hadn't been an easy one. Matt's real father had been a military man, and Matt's early life had been spent at military academies. When his father died and Evelyn married Great-Uncle Henry, he'd stayed in the academy for another year. Then he went on to boarding school, then college, and then service in the Marine Corps, with little chance for parental love in between. Henry was a formidable man himself, and Evelyn was more businesswoman than mother.

But Matt seemed to have gotten enough love from other sources, she thought wryly, remembering the occasional woman she'd seen him with and the adoring glances that came his way. When she was in college, Catherine's girlfriends had begged to come to the ranch, just for a glimpse of Matt.

Catherine pursed her lips and studied Matt's tall, muscular body as he started through the gate. He was devastating physically, all right. And he had Spanish eyes, very dark and sparkling, and a deeply tanned face that was sharp-featured and aristocratic. He was something else. She tingled with pride, just looking at him, although she was ready for a fight if it was going to take one to get out from under his thumb. Part of her knew that Matt would never be able to return her tempestuous feelings for him. And it was because of that, more than anything else, that she had to escape. It was devastating to be around Matt and watch him go out with other women all the time. He seemed to have a different one every month. All of them were experienced, sensual women. Nothing like poor little Kit, who had to hide her tears from him. It would have killed her if he'd known how she really felt—that all her outbursts of anger were just defensive tactics.

"Tomorrow," she whispered, and smiled. "Tomorrow we'll have it out, big cousin."

She lay back and closed her eyes.

The next morning when Catherine came down for breakfast Hal was at the breakfast table with Betty, but Matt was already out the door and gone. Hal looked up, his brown eyes sparkling in a mischievous face. At twenty-three he was the youngest of the three brothers. He was shorter than Matt and not as muscular. Hal had a good brain, when he used it, and was a whiz with machinery. But he preferred the night spots to the ranch and slipped away at every opportunity. He played at life, and Matt had threatened to throw him off the property because of his penchant for playing practical jokes. But he was loveable, for all his wicked ways, and Catherine had a soft spot for him. In her younger days, he'd been her staunchest ally in dodging Matt's temper.

"Hi, cousin!" he grinned. "How was the big city?"

"Great!" She sat down and filled her plate. "I got a job!" She told him all about it, enjoying his amazed look as she talked.

"Have you told Matt?" he asked after a minute, his gaze quietly curious.

"I haven't seen him yet."

Hal pursed his lips. "She doesn't know?" he asked Betty.

Catherine cocked her head at him. "Know what?" she asked hesitantly.

"Matt found out where you really were. He's stopped your allowance."

"Oh, Hal, why did you do that!" Betty groaned.

Catherine's eyes sparkled with passion as she threw down her napkin. "Stopped my allowance? He can't! Those shares are mine!"

"He can do what he likes until you're twenty-five," Hal said.

"Where is he?" Catherine demanded.

"Down on the flats, checking to make sure the cattle were all moved before the rains came," Betty said reluctantly. "He told Hal to get them moved before he left for Houston."

Hal didn't reply. He looked disturbed and reached for his coffee cup.

Catherine didn't notice. She was fuming. She needed that allowance to set herself up in New York. She wouldn't have any money until her first paycheck. And Matt knew it!

"I'll shoot him," she muttered.

"Now, darling, don't be hasty," Betty said, trying to soothe her.

But Catherine was already on her way upstairs to change into jodhpurs and boots.

Chapter Two

The sunlight was wonderful after the thundering flood of late-summer rain the night before, but Catherine wasn't paying the least attention to the beauty of the wide open land and grazing cattle or the distant enormity of the feedlot. Her narrowed green eyes were flashing, and the set of her slender body in the saddle was as rigid as her perfect mouth.

She shivered a little in the early-morning chill. Autumn was coming on. Already the hardwoods were beginning to get crisp leaves on them. She searched the horizon for Matt, but he was nowhere to be seen. She could have screamed. There were times when being part of the Kincaid clan was an absolute torment, and this was one of them. She had a great future in New York in public relations. Why couldn't Matt let her go after it? Of course, he didn't know about the New York job offer, but what he'd done would prevent her from going anywhere without his approval. It was always like that. She made plans and Matt fouled them up. He'd done it for years, and nobody had ever stood up to him. Except Catherine, of course.

This time he wasn't having it all his own way. The fact that he was the chief stockholder in the Kincaid Corporation was irrelevant. Even the fact that she was madly in love with him was irrelevant. He wasn't going to get away with telling her how to live her life.

She spotted movement down on the soggy river flats, where a few red-coated, white-faced Herefords were mired in mud, and she smiled coldly. She saw only a couple of his men, and that was just as well; she didn't really want an audience.

Her heartbeats quickened as she coaxed the little mare into a canter and felt the breeze tossing her straight thick dark hair in the wind.

She looked good in her jodhpurs and in her neat little blue-checked shirt that left her brown arms bare, but it hadn't been for Matthew's sake that she'd dressed so neatly. Matthew wouldn't notice if she did a Lady Godiva unless she scared his precious cattle. He was immune to women, she thought. Freedom was an obsession with Matt. He'd said often enough that the woman hadn't been born who could get him in front of a minister.

Catherine had thought about that. She'd thought about making love to Matt, about feeling his hard sensuous mouth on her own. She'd daydreamed for years about it, about marrying him and living on Comanche Flats forever. But she'd learned over the years to keep her deeper longings to herself. Matt helped by ignoring her occasional stray glance that lingered too long and the quickening of her breath when he came close. She'd dated at college and had brought some of the boys home. To Betty's frank astonishment, Matt had given them a thorough grilling, every one, and he'd set the rules about when Catherine had to be in. It was another of the domineering traits she'd once taken for granted and now resented bitterly. Matt would never want her the way a man wanted a woman. But he had control of her life, and he liked that.

At last she saw him. He was kneeling to examine a hoof of one of the cows. His dark hair was concealed by the wide brim of his hat, and he looked almost like one of the cowboys in his faded denims and chambray shirt and worn boots. But when he stood up, all comparison ended. Matt had the kind of physique that turned up once in a blue moon outside motion pictures. His broad shoulders rippled with muscle, and his lithe body had a sensual rhythm that held women's eyes when he moved. He was long and lean and darkly tanned, and he had eyes so black that they looked like coal. His nose had been broken once or twice and looked it, and his mouth had a perpetual mocking twist that could put Catherine's back up in seconds. His cheekbones were high, a legacy of a Comanche ancestor, and he looked as if he needed a shave even when he didn't because the shadow of his beard was so dark. But he was immaculate for a cattleman. His nails were always trimmed and clean, and he had an arrogant, regal carriage that made Catherine think of the highlander who had come to Texas so many years ago to found the Kincaid line.

The Kincaids had been a political power in this part of the state at one time. Catherine had learned that from listening to Matt's mother talk about Jackson Kincaid, her first husband. She was proud of Matt's lineage and never let him forget it. The Kincaid Corporation, the remnant of a small empire, was Matt's legacy. Evelyn had given shares in it to Great-Uncle Henry, combining both families' interests. But it was Matt who held the power, and nobody forgot it.

Matt's sharp ears caught the sound of her mount's hooves, and he whirled gracefully. His grim face and dark eyes brightened at the look on her face. He tilted his hat back and propped a boot against the oak tree behind him. He leaned back, watching her with an expression that made her want to hit him.

"So there you are," she muttered, fumbling her way out of the saddle.

"Honey, you'll never learn to be a good rider if you don't listen when I try to teach you things. That's no way to come down off a horse,'' he said good-naturedly.

"Don't 'honey' me," she said. She went right up to him, glaring at him, hating him, her small hands clenched at her back. "Mama told me what you've done. Now you listen to me, Matthew Kincaid. I just grew up, and you can stop trying to put me back in your hip pocket. I won't fit! You gave me those shares when I turned eighteen, and you can't take them away."

His narrow eyebrows arched. "Who, me?" he asked innocently. Still watching her with amusement, he pulled a cigarette from his pocket and lit it with maddening carelessness. "I didn't take them away, I just had the interest you were drawing reinvested." He grinned wider. "Look in the small print, Kit. I retained that right when I signed over the shares to you."

Her eyes lanced into him. "What am I going to do to pay my rent in New York, beg on street corners?"

"I don't remember any discussion about New York," he returned at once.

She hated that smile. She knew it all too

well from years past. It meant he'd dug in his heels and there wouldn't be any moving him. Well, she'd just see about that.

"I've been offered a job with a very prestigious New York public relations firm," she told him. "It wasn't easy to get, and it was only because the father of one of my college friends works there that I was even considered. It's a plum of a job, Matt. The salary—"

"You're only twenty-one," he said, pursing his lips. "And New York is a wild place for a little country girl."

"I'm not little!"

His eyes went pointedly to her small breasts, and he grinned. "No?"

She let out a furious cry and aimed a kick at his shins with one hard-booted toe. He sidestepped with lightning grace, and she went down flat on her back in the wet grass and mud.

He grinned at the shock on her face, then flashed a look at two of his men who were riding by with curious looks on their faces.

"Better get up quick, honey, or Ben and Charlie there will think you're trying to entice me into making love to you,'' he said outrageously.

"Matthew...Dane Kincaid...I hate you...!'' she sputtered as she tried to get to her feet.

He was trying to stop laughing, but without much success. His white teeth flashed and black eyes were alive in his swarthy face. He reached down to grab her wrist and jerked her to her feet. His strength was a little frightening. He looked lithe and limber, but he could have forced her to her knees if he'd flexed his hand, and she knew it. Her angry eyes scanned his hard face, her fury kindling all over again at the traces of humor she saw lingering there. She drew back a hand, but it hovered in midair.

"Hold it right there, honey,'' he said, chuckling. "I don't mind a little dirt, but if you connect with that muddy hand, I'll hit you where it hurts most.''

"I'll tell Mama!'' she threatened.

"Betty would hold you still for me.''

He loosed her wrist, and she rubbed it, surprised at the tingling sensation that lingered after his hard fingers had withdrawn.

She tugged her long-tailed shirt out of her

jodhpurs and used the hem of it to wipe off the mud. He stuck his hands on his lean hips and watched her with the infuriating superiority that clung to him like the faint mud stains on his shirt.

She sighed. "I hate you, you know."

"No you don't, Kit." He grinned. "You just want your own way. And this time, you're not getting it. I'd never forgive myself if I turned you loose in that big city all alone, fresh out of college in Forth Worth."

"And that's another sore spot," she threw back at him, shivering a little in the cool air. "You hardly even let me go off to college. Not me, oh no, I had to commute on weekends! It's a wonder you didn't come with me and hold my hand as I crossed streets!"

"I did think about it," he murmured dryly.

"I'm grown up!"

"Not yet," he corrected. His eyes went down to her breasts and lingered there, where the hard tips were visible through her thin shirt, and he smiled slowly. "But you're getting there."

She stared at him unblinkingly, surprised at the remark, at the way he was studying her breasts. Boys had looked at her that way when she wore swimsuits or low-cut blouses, but Matt never had. It shocked her that he'd even bothered to look. Perhaps it was just another way of getting back at her. She folded her arms over her breasts as a scarlet flush covered her cheeks. She avoided meeting his eyes.

"Hey," he commanded softly.

"What?"

"Look at me."

She forced her embarrassed eyes up, but he wasn't teasing her. He looked faintly kind, for Matt.

"If you want to practice public relations, I'll put you to work," he said. "You can publicize my foundation sale month after next."

"Matt, that's not a job!"

"It's a job," he said firmly. "A lot of work goes into that annual sale, and a lot depends on its being a success. I usually hire an outside agency to handle it, but since you're here, you can do it. I'll even let you design the brochure." He eyed her closely. "That's a challenge, honey. Show me how capable you are, and I'll make you a present of an apartment in New York and find you another job to boot. I've got some contacts of my own.''

She wavered. It was tempting. Very tempting. And if he hadn't been trying to bend her to his will, she might have accepted his offer. But he was calling the shots, and if she made a success of the job, he'd probably find some way to make her keep working for him. She'd never get away.

So, he wanted his sale publicized, did he? She smiled faintly. Okay. She'd do it. And in such a way that he'd be more than delighted to send her on her way.

"Okay," she agreed after a minute, her green eyes sparkling. "I'll just take that dare."

"I'll start you off tomorrow morning. Be at the office, eight-thirty sharp," he replied. "Now you'd better get home and change into something a little more decent, or Betty will come after me with a shotgun."

"I can just see you now, running for the border," she returned dryly.

He smiled wickedly. "This far away?" he said with a chuckle. "Hell, no, I'd drive." He pulled his hat low over his eyes. "Hadn't you better go home and change?"

She knew when she was defeated. Green eyes glared up at him. "You're just stifling me," she ground out. "Smothering me! My gosh, you tie me to the house. You grill every man I date. You won't let me go to New York and find my own way in life—Matt, I'm a grown woman," she said, trying to reason with him. "You're an old bachelor…!"

His eyebrows lifted as he lit another cigarette. "Honey, I'm just thirty-one."

"And someday you'll be fifty-one and all alone, and what will you do then?" she asked haughtily.

He smiled slowly. "I guess I'll start seducing kids your age."

She opened her mouth, started to speak, thought better of it and closed her mouth with a snap.

"My, my, the fish aren't biting today," he said conversationally. Boldly, his dark eyes wandered slowly down the length of her slender body, assessing her; then suddenly they shot up to catch her eyes. She stared back, and the world narrowed to Matt's face. Cows bellowed all around and cowboys whistled and called, moving them along, but she no longer noticed them. A wild tingling feeling raced through her body as she studied Matt. Never before had she looked at him so intently.

He touched the cigarette to his chiseled mouth, breaking the spell. "No comeback, Kit?" he murmured dryly.

She sighed. "I can't fight you," she muttered. "You just laugh at me."

"It's less dangerous than doing what I'd like," he returned, his dark eyes sparkling.

"Try slinging me over your knee, cattle baron, and I'll make you a legend in your own time with that brochure you want drawn up," she threatened.

"No you won't." He threw down the cigarette and ground it out. "We're buddies, remember?"

"We used to be. Then you started being so horrible to me," she reminded him. She dusted off her stained jodhpurs. "God knows what I'll tell Mama about the way I look," she added, giving him a mischievous glance.

"Tell her you tried to seduce me," he suggested with a wicked grin.

"That'll be the day," she said darkly, turning back toward her horse.

"Don't you think you could?" he teased.

She mounted, feeling odd at the suggestion, and glanced down at him. "Actually," she told him, "I don't know how."

"No experience?" he asked mockingly, but there was a serious note in his deep, drawling voice.

"I've been saving myself for you, didn't you know?"

He laughed softly. "Have you?"

It was new and heady to flirt openly with Matt. She'd never done it before. She wrapped the reins gently around one hand and stilled the nervous little mare, patting her neck as she talked softly to her. Her amused eyes met Matt's. "Better lock your door at night."

His dark eyes twinkled with new lights. "I do. I've been terrified of you since you graduated from high school."

"Have you really?" She grinned. "I did notice all the women you gathered around you to protect yourself from me."

He didn't smile. His eyes narrowed thoughtfully. "Your suitors have been conspicuous by their absence the past few months," he remarked.

She lifted her shoulders. "Jack gave me up in the early summer," she said. "He was afraid you'd kill him if he tried anything with me. He even said so."

He looked toward the cowboys, who were starting to drive cattle through a nearby opening in the fence. "I've got work to do, honey."

"Conference over." She sighed. "You never talk to me."

He looked up, and something in his black eyes made her nervous. "I may do that— sooner than you think, little Kit." His gaze grew piercing, searching. "After all, you're straining at the bonds for the first time. You'll fly away if I'm not careful."

"I'm not a bird, you know," she said pleasantly.

"More of a tadpole," he murmured.

"You call me a frog again, and I'll tell Hal and Jerry," she threatened.

"Tadpole, not frog. Go ahead and tell them," he challenged, smiling. "Remember me, Kit? I'm the black sheep."

"Some black sheep. You're the one with the brains and the strong back," she had to admit, softening as she looked down at him. His face was creased with harsh lines that neither of his brothers had. It was always Matt who'd had the lion's share of the responsibility. Hal did what he pleased, and Jerry did what he could, but he didn't have Matt's business sense and was intelligent enough to admit it.

"Was I asking for a vote of confidence?" he asked with mock astonishment.

"You never would. But you've got mine," she said with a soft smile.

He seemed to tauten at the softness in her voice. "Risky, Kit, looking at me that way," he said with a faint smile. "I might go crazy right here."

"You, go crazy over a woman?" she asked with a laugh. "That'll be the day. Anyway, it would take someone with experience and pizzazz. I'm just your pesky stepcousin."

"You're a beauty, young Catherine," he returned, and seemed to really mean it. She colored gently at the masculine appreciation in the look he gave her. "Quality, all the way."

"You're not bad yourself, cowboy," she

murmured demurely. "I have to go home and change. I thought I'd go see a movie later."

"Did you? What kind of movie?"

"There's one of those very adult shows at the drive-in," she confided. "I thought I'd take Hal and educate him."

His face went hard all at once, and the sudden eclipse of humor surprised her. "No," he said quietly. "Not Hal. If you go to any drive-ins, I'll take you. And not tonight. I've got a date already. I'll take you Friday."

It was like sticking her finger in an electric socket. She simply stared at him. "What?"

"I said I'll take you to the movies Friday, Kit," he replied, and grinned at her. "I'm not letting you corrupt Hal. Besides, he's too young for you."

She burst out laughing. She must have imagined his sudden anger, she told herself. Matt had only been teasing all along.

"I suppose he is," she had to admit. "Are you?"

His mouth curled. "What do you think, honey?" he asked in a tone he'd never used with her before. It was like velvet. Soft. Honey smooth. Seductive.

She stared down at him curiously. "You're too old for drive-ins," she said slowly.

He shook his head. "We'll take the pickup and I'll buy you a pizza. It will rejuvenate me," he added with a grin.

"I can just see you at a drive-in," she murmured. Her green eyes flirted with his dark ones. "Okay. But I won't kiss you if you drink beer."

His eyebrows lifted and something flashed in his eyes. He laughed gently. "Okay."

She'd shocked herself with her impulsive remark, and now she felt embarrassed. As if Matt would want to kiss her! But her eyes fell to his hard mouth as if of their own accord, and she stared at his lips with unexpected curiosity. She looked up in time to see a wildness in his eyes. A shock of electric current linked them, making her want to dive down into his arms and kiss his hard, sexy mouth until the aching of her young body stopped. And that shocked her enough that she dragged her eyes away.

"You did mean what you said, about letting me go to New York if I do a good job on your sale?" she persisted.

He turned back toward his men. "I meant it."

"Matt—"

"Hey, Charlie, bring the truck for this one!" he called to an old cowboy and he gestured toward a downed cow farther along the trail.

She sighed in irritation. Well, that was that, he'd just forgotten that she was alive. That was his response to discussions he didn't want. He just walked away from them. She glared at his back for a long moment before she suddenly wheeled her mount and started toward the ranch.

Well, at least she had a chance to escape now. Her face burned as she remembered what she'd said to him about the drive-in. She'd probably shocked him with that silly remark about kissing him.

She shifted in the saddle, thinking about going to a drive-in with Matt. Her body tingled with delight at the prospect. He'd never taken her anywhere alone. And probably he wasn't going to now, either. He'd invite one of the family to go with them. And why would he take the pickup?

Matt bothered her. He puzzled her. He was a cutup, a wild man—except when he was being Mr. Kincaid. She'd seen him do that. She'd watched him put down men who thought they could walk all over him because he seemed easygoing. There was a white-hot temper and a will like iron underneath his good humor.

Worrying about things wasn't going to help, she told herself. She'd do better to concentrate on how to promote the cattle sale. It was her only chance of escape from her family. And from Matt. She couldn't spend the rest of her life waiting for him. She couldn't live near him and watch him marry someone else—and he would eventually. The corporation would have to have an heir, and he was in control. Probably it would be some sophisticated socialite with holdings of her own. A merger more than a marriage.

She leaned forward over the little mare's mane and gave her her head as they went toward the barn.

Chapter Three

Jerry and Barrie were at supper that night. Jerry, like Hal and Matt, had dark eyes, but he alone of the three had sandy-blond hair and a receding hairline. He was taller than Hal, but not as tall as Matt. Barrie was redheaded and blue eyed and very petite and mischievous. Catherine had always adored her.

As Annie waddled in with the salads, Catherine allowed Hal to seat her, and she noted his thoughtful glances. Matt hadn't made an appearance yet, and Catherine found herself watching the doorway, waiting. She knew he was going out, that he wouldn't be joining them for the evening meal, but she couldn't help watching for him. Habits were hard to break. She looked down at her blue shirtwaist dress and imagined I Adore Matt written all over it with a felt-tip marker. That was vaguely amusing and she laughed.

"That's better," Hal murmured. "You were looking solemn, little cousin."

"Who, me?" She gaped. "I'm never solemn."

"I know," he returned.

"Betty said you were trying to go to New York to work," Jerry said, glancing at her. He smiled absently. "I knew you'd only come to grief."

"How?"

"I know my brother. Matt keeps you on a short leash, doesn't he?"

Catherine glared at him. "I can do what I please. As it happens," she said to save face, "Matt's offered me a job. I'm organizing the foundation sale."

"Darling, how lovely!" Barrie exclaimed. "You'll do a grand job."

"You and your cattle hang-up," Jerry growled at her. "I can see you now, leading that prize bull of yours around, with the baby under one arm—when you ever decide to have a baby.''

"Don't be silly, my love,'' Barrie murmured, peering up at him. "I'll have the baby in one of those carry things they wear these days. He'll learn the business from the ground up.'' She elbowed her husband. "Anyway, what do you mean, 'when I decide to have a baby'? How can I? You're never at home. It takes two,'' she added with a poisonous smile.

Jerry cleared his throat and offered Betty the rolls.

Catherine and Hal exchanged amused glances just as Matt walked in. It was obvious he'd changed for his date, because he was wearing a dark dinner jacket with a red tie. He looked so devastating that Catherine had to drop her eyes.

"Hal, I'd like a word with you,'' he said without preamble.

Hal looked uncomfortable and made a face, but he got up and went with his stern older brother out into the hall. The door closed and everyone exchanged puzzled glances.

"He didn't move those cattle like Matt told

him,'' Barrie volunteered with a grimace. ''At least four of them drowned.''

So that was what Matt had been doing on the flats, Catherine thought suddenly, amazed that she hadn't connected the mired cattle with Hal's disobedience. Poor old Hal, she thought. Matt would eat him alive.

''Will he ever grow up?'' Jerry grumbled. ''He plays at life.''

''He's very young, dear,'' Betty intervened.

Catherine was just about to rush to his defense, too, just as a loud voice broke the silence in the hall, followed by a thump and a hard thud. Catherine jumped to her feet and opened the door to find Hal just picking himself up from the floor. Matt was standing over him, unruffled, his face like stone, his eyes blazing with anger. He glanced at Catherine, and he was a stranger again, all authority and bristling masculinity. He laughed curtly.

''Florence Nightingale to the rescue,'' he chided. ''Pick him up and pet him, if you like, but do it damned fast. He's leaving for Houston. And if he doesn't straighten out his priorities while he's there,'' he added with a cold glare at Hal, who was gingerly touching his jaw, "he can damned well stay in Houston."

"My God, it was only four head—" Hal began.

"One head would have been one too many," Matt replied.

"Jerry and I have a stake in the corporation too," Hal shot back. "You're not the whole show!"

"I am until you can carry your share of the load," Matt returned. "Grow up!"

Hal got to his feet and glared at the taller man. "The iron man, aren't you?" He laughed mirthlessly. "No chinks in your armor, no human weaknesses. Not even a weakness for a special woman."

"You'd better phone and see if you can get a flight out of here tonight," Matt said, ignoring the little speech.

Hal inclined his head. "Whatever you say, boss." He fingered his jaw and glanced ruefully at Catherine. "Be sure to duck, cousin."

Catherine watched him turn toward the stairs. She started back toward the dining room, but Matt caught her arm.

The light touch was indescribable. He came

up behind her and was so close that she could hear his heavy breath as it sighed out over her hair. His fingers were steely through the soft jersey of her dress sleeve, and she couldn't seem to get her breath.

Someone had closed the door to the dining room after she'd gone through it. Probably Jerry, she thought dazedly; he wasn't one to eavesdrop.

"Afraid of me?" he asked at her back.

She turned and looked up at him with soft green eyes. "No. Not really. It's just that you seem like a stranger sometimes, Matt."

"Hal has to learn responsibility," he said.

"I won't argue that," she replied. "But he won't ever be you."

He sighed half-angrily. His dark eyes searched hers in the sudden stillness of the hall.

"Don't you have a date to rush off to?" she asked pointedly.

"I have a social engagement," he replied. He pulled out a gold cigarette case—the one she'd given him for Christmas last year—and casually lit a cigarette, as if he had all the time in the world.

"Same difference," she said.

He shook his head, then lifted the cigarette to his smiling mouth. "It's a formal dinner. And women weren't included, except for the wives of the organizers."

"You don't owe me any explanations, Matt." She started toward the dining room, but he drew her back with the lightest pressure of his fingers.

"No, I don't," he agreed. She stared at his red tie.

His fingers moved to her throat and stroked its soft elegant line, and her mouth trembled. She looked up at him with her breath sticking in her throat.

"Don't," she pleaded breathlessly. It was the first time he'd ever touched her like that, and it frightened her. All her wild dreams went into hiding at the reality. The uncontrolled pleasure she felt was unexpected.

"Why not?" he murmured. "Bachelors are entitled to play a little, honey," he said with a slow smile, and his fingers stroked over a larger area, edging under the neck of her dress and onto her shoulder.

"Not with me, you don't," she said. She

reached up to catch his fingers. "It's not fair, Matt. Shooting fish in a barrel."

"Why not, when it's the only way you can get the fish at all?"

"Matt..."

He looked down at her soft, full mouth, outlined carefully with a delicate lipstick. He moved closer, the hand that held the cigarette sliding around her waist to draw her body to the length of his.

She couldn't breathe at all now. She looked up into dark, secretive eyes and felt her body begin to throb. He'd held her before, of course, to comfort her when she cried and once to carry her over a rising stream bed. He'd even carried her to bed once when she was sick. But it had never been like this before, with his dark eyes hungry as they looked into hers and a nameless awareness between them that grew by the second.

"Have you ever been kissed properly?" he asked in a deep, gruff whisper.

Her lips parted under a rush of breath. "Of... course."

"I like it hard," he whispered, bending his

head. "I may be rough with you at first. Don't be frightened."

"Matt!" Her voice sounded wild.

His fingers tilted her chin, and there was a sensuality in his face that she'd never seen before. "What are you so nervous about?" he breathed against her lips.

Her mouth felt the threat of his, and her hands clenched on his lapels as the images in her mind overwhelmed her. Her body was trembling, and he was so close to her that he had to feel it.

"So hungry," he whispered, threatening her mouth with his without ever coming close enough to take it. "Aching for me. And all it would take is another fraction of an inch, like this," he whispered, moving his head down so that she could breathe the minty scent of him, "and I could have you, Kit...."

"Please," she whimpered, stiffening as the words and his cologne and the warmth of his whipcord body all weakened her. "Matt, please, please..." She didn't realize that she was reaching up, her cold and trembling hands at the nape of his neck, her body at fever pitch with wanting.

"Oh, no," he laughed softly. Both hands caught her by the waist. "Not yet."

Her eyes widened. She was shaking. Shaking! And he was smiling at her with such worldly amusement....

"Damn you," she said under her breath, tears threatening.

"I'm late already," he said. "Go eat your dinner, honey. We'll put everything on hold until tomorrow night. The movie," he reminded her in a low whisper. "And I won't drink beer."

"I won't go!" She stared at him, eyes enormous in her face, her body shaking with what he'd aroused and not satisfied.

"Yes you will." He brushed back a strand of chestnut hair from her shoulder. His eyes held hers.

She moved away from him, fighting for composure. "I won't be just one in a line," she said. "I won't let you seduce me. You're just after a new thrill. And I'm not going to be it," she said firmly.

He laughed deep in his throat, and his eyes were bright with amusement. "Coward," he murmured dryly.

She flushed, and almost ran back into the dining room. Catching herself, she slowly opened the door and left him standing in the hall.

Catherine didn't hear another word that was said to her for the rest of the night. She smiled and talked automatically, and all the while she felt Matt's hands, the sigh of his breath on her mouth. She ached all over with strange new hungers, feeling oddly restless and irritable. And in the morning she was going to have to pretend she felt nothing because Matt was astute and it would be suicide to let him see how she felt. If only she knew what kind of game he was playing! Would he really go that far? Would he tease her just to keep her under his thumb? She lay awake until the early hours, worrying about it, more determined than ever to break free before she fell victim to his dark, sensuous charm.

Hal flew out sometime in the night and wasn't at the breakfast table the next morning. Betty was, though. And Matt.

He watched Catherine over his second cup of coffee, his eyes mocking as she fumbled her way through bacon and eggs.

"Such a lovely day, after all that rain," Betty was saying. "I think I'll drive into Fort Worth and do some shopping. Catherine, can I pick up anything for you?"

"No, thank you, Mama," Catherine replied, trying to stop her renegade heart from running wild every time Matt looked in her direction. He was wearing a three-piece gray suit, and he looked debonair and worldly.

She had on a simple short-sleeved green knit top and a skirt, and was worried that she might be overdressed for her first day on the job. "I didn't know what to wear this morning," she began hesitantly.

"Angel and the other girls usually wear dresses or skirts," Matt told her. "Jack, our sales manager, wears a suit. I alternate between suits and jeans, depending on my schedule. Today I have to fly down to San Antonio, so I'm a bit more formal. But we don't have a dress code. You can wear jeans if you like."

"I'll remember tomorrow. Do I get my own office?" she asked with a smile.

"You can share mine, honey. I've got an extra desk." He finished his coffee. "Ready?"

"Yes. See you later, Mama," she murmured, rising as Matt held her chair. She couldn't help but be puzzled by his new polite behavior. Even Betty seemed to notice, but she only smiled.

It felt strange riding beside Matt in his Lincoln. He glanced at her curiously; it wasn't like her to be so silent, so subdued.

"What's wrong?" he asked gently as he pulled up in front of the ranch office.

"Nothing," she said quickly and gave him a flashing smile. "I was just thinking up ideas for the sale."

Fortunately, he took that at face value. He got out and opened her door, but he paused when she expected him to move, so that she cannoned into him.

His hands, firm and strong, caught her shoulders and he was so close that she felt his breath in her hair. He smelled of spice and tobacco, and the muscular warmth of his body enveloped her from head to toe. She couldn't quite breathe, and she didn't dare look up. Her heart was beating like mad.

"You've avoided looking at me all morning," he said quietly. "Is it because I tried to kiss you...or because I stopped too soon?"

Her face burned in reaction. And still she couldn't look up. Her lips parted on a rush of breath. "It's...new."

"Yes."

"Matt..."

"What?"

"Just...Matt." She lifted her face then, and her misty green eyes sought his. He seemed to stop breathing and just stared at her. He didn't smile. His eyes searched, probed.

"Don't be afraid of me, Kit," he said, his voice deep and slow and soft.

"You're a stranger...."

He shook his head. "No. You're just looking at me in a different way."

"Why?" she asked, needing to know.

His hands tightened on her shoulders. "One day at a time, honey," he said then. "Don't ask questions until you want the answers. Let's get to work."

He turned her and prodded her toward the big one-story building that housed an impressive computer set-up. He had four young women working for him and two salesmen. Hal, when he was in town, had his own office as well. It was a smoothly run operation.

Thousands of dollars' worth of cattle were bought and sold without a single head being moved physically. Matt even had cattle on video cassettes so he could show them to prospective buyers out of town. It was a wildly progressive kind of business, and Matt ran it with ease.

He showed her into his private, carpeted office. The room looked like it belonged to Matt, all tough leather and earth colors and hardwood. There were two desks: his and a smaller one, where a computer and printer sat.

"You know how to use this, don't you?" he asked, smiling amusedly.

She glared up at him. "Yes. I had one just like it at school."

His eyes dropped to her mouth, and she was glad there were other girls working here. It kept him from doing what she really wanted him to do.

"If you have any problems with the computer, Angel can help you. She's the brunette at the desk outside my office. She has the preliminary information on the sale, as well. Until I volunteered you, it was her job to get it together for the public relations people. Okay?"

"Okay." She sat down and stared at the keyboard, a hundred conflicting emotions making her restless, disturbing her. She was hot despite the air conditioning. It was already late September, but the weather was getting hotter instead of colder, if today was any indication.

"Don't wear your hair like that tonight," he said suddenly.

She glanced up, remembering that she had her chestnut waves in a bun on top of her head. "What?"

"Leave it loose. I hate hairpins."

"Do you ever stop giving orders?" she asked.

"Sure. In bed."

Her face flushed, and he smiled—a sensual, confident smile that frightened her a little. He was a predator, and she was the quarry. That was what she'd always thought she wanted, but now that it was happening, she was afraid.

"Anyway," she continued nervously, "I'm not sure I want to go to a drive-in with you."

"Yes, you do," he returned. He leaned over her, surrounding her, one hand on her chair, the other on the edge of the desk. His dark face was close to hers, and she could see the hard lines in it, the twist of his firm lips, the silver sprinkled in the darkness of his straight, thick hair. His cheek was very close, and she wanted to touch its hardness.

Her eyes lifted to his and got lost there. She saw the muscles in his jaw go taut as they stared at each other, and his breathing began to get ragged.

"I want your mouth, Catherine," he said unexpectedly. "So I think I'd better get out of here before I shock a few people."

He stood up, and she fumbled with the papers on the desk, feeling all thumbs and inexperience while she tried to decide if she'd just been hearing things or if he'd really said what she thought she'd heard.

"I'll, uh, get started," she said in a husky voice.

"You do that." He stuck his hands in his pockets, reading the flash of uncertainty on her face. "Catherine, I won't hurt you," he said under his breath.

She really crimsoned then, and he sauntered out of the office, catching other pairs of eyes as he walked. He really was the most devastating man!

What was she going to do? She wanted him so much. There had never really been anyone in her heart except Matt though the only interest he'd ever shown in her before was to check out the competition. He seemed to accept it as a necessity, but he made it as uncomfortable as he could for her few dates.

She wondered at the extent of his possessiveness. He'd worked his way into her life so slowly that, before she'd realized it, he'd become her life. And he knew it. That was what hurt most, that he had her in the palm of his hand while he was still going out with a string of women. He didn't even make a secret of it. Because, she told herself, he never got serious. He wouldn't get serious about her, either. She'd have to keep that in mind in case she got stupid and started begging him to kiss her at the drive-in.

For the time being, she decided to concentrate all her energy on preparing the publicity she would get out for Matt's foundation sale. And that meant she needed a list of the lots of cattle he was going to sell. She pulled them out of the computer, complete with herd numbers, lineage, weights and gaining ratios. It was a complicated business, cattle raising, but Catherine knew enough about it to get by.

She worked out a set of dates for releasing information and got together a list of potential out-of-state buyers to contact, all her tumultuous feelings forgotten in her fascination with her new job. Then she went to find Matt.

"If you're looking for Matt, he's already gone," Angel sighed, chin in her hands as she stared wistfully at the door. "He's flying down to San Antonio with his lunch date. I'll bet it's that Laredo real estate agent again," she murmured. "She's been hanging around for a month. Well, at least she's better than the oil company executive lady from New Orleans," she added with a bright smile.

"I didn't know there was a current lady," Catherine said, trying to sound lighthearted. "We never see them at the house."

"I don't imagine so!" Angel said meaningfully. "We only know because they call him here. This last one has been around for about three months. But I think he's getting tired of her. He's been dodging her calls all week."

It was a horrible reminder of what would happen to her if she let Matt get too close, of what would happen when he tired of her innocence. He wasn't a marrying man; he'd said so. That only left one thing he could want, and after last night, she knew she was on the endangered-species list. That almost-kiss had knocked her to her knees. She could barely imagine what it would be like if he started making love to her.

And tonight he was going to take her to a drive-in, and she was going to go under in a haze if he touched her. She had to find an excuse not to go. The real estate agent from Laredo could have him, she thought venomously. She didn't care!

Catherine returned to her desk and turned the computer back on. She entered more information onto the disk, then hit the wrong keys. The program disk crashed before her startled eyes and she felt herself caving in. What a beautiful way to start a new job!

"Angel," she called sweetly.

The older girl stuck her head around the doorway with a grin. "Problems?"

"Uh, do you happen to have a spare program disk?" Catherine asked.

Angel grinned. "I did that my first day. Now I don't feel so alone. Back in a jiffy."

Catherine started all over again, furious with Matt for his attitude toward her when all the time he was seeing another woman. She glared at the screen and smiled slowly. Well, she did want to go to New York, didn't she? And if she failed at this, she was sure to get there even quicker. Matt's anger would be a minor obstacle, but she'd face it when she had to. With a wicked smile, she began to alter the names of the cattle. Only a little, of course. Names like "Comanche Flats Mile High #42" to "Comanche Flats Mule High #42." And then there was "Black Gold #20" to "Black Mold #20." When she got to the part about each bull's sire and dam, it got better . "This young bull's mother was the lovely Comanche Flats debutante heifer Miss Standish #10, who early in life married the dashing Comanche Flats bull Mr. Struts."

She had to close the door to Matt's office to keep Angel from overhearing her wild giggles as she entered the information for the brochure. Well, Matt wanted something catchy, didn't he? What a surprise this would be!

Chapter Four

Catherine spent the rest of the day hiding in laughter. But she kept thinking ahead to the night and tingled all over. Waves of feeling like nothing she'd ever experienced in her life were buffeting her. She wanted Matt with a fever. She wanted Matt so much that even remembering the Laredo real estate agent didn't faze her. She wasn't a shrinking violet, after all. She had a few things going for her, too. And if last night was any indication, Matt wasn't exactly immune to her. That gave her an edge.

He hadn't come back when it was quitting time, so Catherine hitched a ride back up to the house with Angel. There was a note from Betty saying she'd gone into town to visit Mrs. Guthrie, one of her friends, and would be late. Annie always visited her sister on Friday night, so she wasn't there. Hal was in Houston. With a sigh, Catherine wondered if Matt would be back tonight, and since she hadn't heard otherwise, she assumed he would.

Since he'd said they were going to a movie, she dressed casually in a soft lavender silk blouse that buttoned and a striped lavender, burgundy and gray wraparound skirt. She left her hair long, brushing it until it fell softly and silkily around her face and shoulders. She stared at herself, liking what she saw. Now, if only Matt liked what he saw...

It was after six when he came home. He looked tired for once, but his eyes darkened and twinkled when he saw Catherine.

"Nice," he murmured deeply.

She curtsied. "I had my body designed just to please you," she said with a laugh.

A smile crossed his tired face. "Butterfly," he said. "You color the world, Kit."

"Flowery speeches? Why, Mr. Kincaid, I didn't know you had it in you."

"Let me shower and change," he murmured as he came closer, "and I'll show you what else I've got."

"Promises, promises," she said coquettishly.

He smiled and turned toward the stairs. "I'll hurry so we don't miss the first show," he said. "Any particular thing you want to *not* see? If I don't drink beer, that is?" he added mischievously.

She flushed to her hairline, hating the ease with which he disconcerted her. "I like science fiction," she mumbled.

"So do I. Okay, we'll see that new picture at the Grand that they're raving about."

It was a chilly night, and she was glad she'd worn a sweater, but Matt turned on the heater in the big new pickup truck, and it was toasty warm. He looked nice, she thought as he pulled into a parking space at the drive-in. He was wearing new jeans with a patterned blue shirt and shiny tan boots and a cream Stetson, and he looked so sexy that her hands itched to touch him.

He seemed to know that, and the sideways

look he gave her as he reached out for the speaker said it all. She quickly averted her eyes to the screen. Previews were showing.

He turned up the sound, and she made a pretense of listening, but all the while all she could hear was the sound of her own wild heartbeat. Why was he taking her to a movie, when he'd spent years keeping her at arms' length? Was it because she was trying to get out from under his thumb, and this was some new way he'd thought up to keep her at Comanche Flats?

"How about some pizza?" he asked.

"Can I have that and coffee, too?" she asked.

"Whatever you want, Kit," he murmured, watching her with eyes that promised heaven.

She blushed helplessly as she looked back at him, a pirate sitting there with his sensuous mouth smiling at her, his dark eyes mischievous, teasing.

"Greenhorn," he chuckled. "Are you afraid of me?"

"I'd like that coffee," she sidestepped.

"Come on, then." He slid toward her so

they could get out on her side and not have to put the speaker up again.

She got out, and he followed, taking her hand in his as they walked down the lot to the concession stand. Her fingers tingled as they locked with his big ones, and she felt very feminine and smug as they walked into the roomy snack bar. Especially when she saw other young women coveting him.

One particular woman, a striking blonde, was really giving him the eye. And, incredibly, he ignored her.

Catherine stared up at him uncomprehendingly as he ordered coffee and pizza.

He glanced down and tugged her closer with an arm around her waist. "Why so puzzled, Kit?" he murmured.

She shifted, her gaze going helplessly to the blonde, who'd given up and moved away with her date, a tall lanky youth who couldn't hold a candle to Matt's rough sensuality.

Matt's hand squeezed her waist. "Do I really strike you as the kind of man who flirts with other women when he's out on a date?" he asked curiously.

She stared at his broad chest. "No. I'm

sorry. But she was so lovely," she added, smiling.

"Not half as lovely as you are. Is that what you wanted to hear?"

"You don't have to flatter me."

He studied her averted face as the waitress brought their pizza. "Later, young Kit, you're going to eat those words. I promise."

Her body tingled with the threat of a revenge sweeter than her wildest dreams. She couldn't meet his eyes as they went back to the truck.

"Why the truck?" she asked when they were safely inside eating pizza.

"It's got vinyl seats," he said with a grin. "You don't think I'm going to eat pizza in that velour-covered dream of a Lincoln I drive on business?"

"Silly old me," she mumbled with a wicked smile.

"Besides," he added, sipping coffee to wash down the last of his pizza, "the Lincoln's front seat is smaller than this cab."

She frowned up at him. "What difference does that make?"

He lifted an eyebrow and chuckled softly. "I couldn't stretch out in it."

"Oh." She still didn't understand, and he was laughing more uproariously by the minute.

"It has something to do with not drinking beer...?" he prodded.

Her face burned, but she didn't drop her indignant eyes. "Now see here, Matthew Dane Kincaid!"

"Well, honey, you were the one who started it," he reminded her. He swept off his Stetson and looped it into a hat carrier above the rearview mirror. "I didn't have a thought in my mind until you told me you wouldn't kiss me if I drank beer. And I've gone dry all day in the heat, just thinking about it."

"I never know when to take you seriously," she said, defeated by his wide grin.

"Yes. I like it that way." He slid his arm across the back of the seat and stared at her as the feature film's opening credits flashed across the big screen. The light spilling from the screen accentuated the planes and curves of Matt's handsome face and the odd look in his narrowed eyes. "Come here, Kit."

Her heart stopped as she stared back at him, her face soft and hesitant, showing just a little fear of the stranger beside her.

"Come on," he coaxed. "I won't kiss you until you want me to."

"You're the most dreadful tease," she muttered to disguise the throbbing hunger of her body. She slid across the seat, stiffening a little as his arm went around her shoulders with lazy carelessness. Seconds later, when his arm remained still and warm, and the clean spicy scent of his body settled around her, she relaxed and let her cheek rest against his broad shoulder.

She watched the screen and saw nothing. Matt's lean, strong fingers kept brushing her neck and her cheek and her hair, and she tingled from the contact while she tried to decide if it was accidental or deliberate. Whatever it was, her pulse was going wild.

She turned her face so that she could see his, and he looked down at her in the semi-darkness. His fingers brushed the side of her neck again, then suddenly pressed lightly against the visible throb of her pulse.

Her breath stopped. She was hungry for

him, and now he knew how hungry. His other hand went under her chin and gently cupped it, and his head bent toward hers.

She stopped breathing altogether. The people on the big screen were suddenly screaming as a creature emerged from part of a spaceship, but Catherine didn't even hear them. All she heard was the soft sigh of Matt's smoky breath as his mouth brushed lightly against hers.

His fingers closed about her cheeks, parting her lips, and slowly he took them under his for the first time. Her breath caught as she felt the texture of his hard, warm mouth, the slight bristly pressure where his shaven cheek touched her skin. She savored the expert firmness of his lips as he began to deepen the kiss.

Her hands went hesitantly to his shirt front and stopped there as she tried to decide what to do with them.

Matt lifted his mouth and held it poised over hers like a heady threat. "I'm not wearing an undershirt," he whispered outrageously. "If you want to touch me, go ahead."

It was too much too soon, and she stiffened. He laughed softly, as if her uncertainty delighted him.

"Virgin," he whispered, brushing his mouth lightly against hers. "Virgin. I feel as if I've never made love before, never tasted a woman's mouth or wanted her hands on me. You make it new for me, Kit."

"You know a lot," she whispered as his teeth nipped her earlobe and made her pulse jump.

"Of course I know a lot. I'm thirty-one." His fingers slid up and down her throat caressingly. "Hold me, Kit."

He helped her, sliding her arms up and around his neck, bringing her close so that her breasts slid softly against his hard chest. Her blouse was thin, and there was no bra under it—sheer idiocy on her part, she knew, because his own shirt was thin and he had to be able to feel her.

He did. He stiffened. His hands stilled on her back and his mouth opened against her forehead.

"My God, you're soft," he whispered roughly.

She wasn't experienced enough to handle a remark like that. She nuzzled her face into his throat and clung, while his hands slid to her rib cage and ran up and down it, his thumbs edging out to find that softness and explore it in the hot, pulsating silence.

His breath was audible as his mouth went down on hers. He held the kiss a long moment, dragging his lips roughly against hers when she began to respond to him with shy abandon.

"If you'll move away a little, I can touch you," he whispered into her mouth. "I want that. I want to take you in my hands and see just how soft you are."

She trembled and he felt it. His hands moved slowly to her back and smoothed up and down it in long, aching sweeps, while his mouth found her cheek and then her ear.

"Okay," he murmured gently, "I'll slow down." He drew back to look at her, his eyes soft and amused. "Just how green are you?"

She shifted in his loose embrace. "Well..."

"Come on."

Her mutinous mouth pouted as she looked up at him. "It's your fault. Mama never would let me go out with the experienced boys, and you always took her side against me."

"Of course I did," he said. "Do I look stupid?"

"What I got left with were boys who didn't know any more than I did," she said, then sighed. "That is no way to get educated," she added, glaring.

"I'll do the educating," he said, and he didn't sound as if he were teasing at all. He tilted her chin up and searched her eyes for a long time. "No experience at all?"

"Not really," she confessed. "A French kiss is about as intimate as it ever got, and I think I must be frigid anyway, because I hated it."

He smiled. He chuckled. He caught her hand when she tried to hit him.

"No fair," he murmured. "You'll hurt my feelings."

"You don't have feelings," she shot back. "You're laughing at me; that's all you ever do is…oh!"

His mouth had stopped the snowballing tirade. She started to hit him, then felt his tongue enter her mouth and she froze. Her eyes opened to find his open, too. He was watching her reaction. His eyes were dark and smoldering, and his tongue was doing the wildest things to her mouth. She gasped. Her hands caught his shoulders and clung bruisingly; her heart seemed to stop beating.

She couldn't help it: she went under. Her eyes closed on a wild little moan and her nails stabbed into him rhythmically like the paws of a kitten in a pleasured daze.

He moved her so that she was lying across him with her head in the crook of his arm. And while the kiss made her crazy, his fingers began a slow, tender progression up her rib cage. They moved up just to a soft curve of her breast and then down again, in a lazy teasing pattern that managed eventually to make her arch and cry out in frustration.

Her eyes opened as he finally released her mouth to look into her flushed, surrendered face.

"I thought you didn't like French kisses," he mused.

"It's different when you do it," she whispered back, wonder in the look she gave him.

"I know how," he said simply. His fingers went back up her body again. "I know how to do this, too. And when you're half out of your mind wanting it, I'll touch you."

"I already am half out of my mind," she

said shakily. Her whole body trembled this time when his fingers started back down to her waist again. "Are you trying...to make me beg?"

He shook his head. "I'm not into ego trips. This," he whispered, emphasizing his words with another achingly slow trailing of his fingertips against the blouse, "makes the pleasure so much sweeter when it happens. There's nothing sensuous about being grabbed."

"I've never been...grabbed."

"I know." He bent and kissed the very tip of her nose. "Why didn't you wear a bra, Catherine?" he asked softly. "Were you afraid it might discourage me?"

Her lips parted as she looked up at him, helpless, hungry. "I didn't think at all." Her eyes searched his slowly, her breath ragged as he delicately began to increase the area his fingers were tantalizing. "Matt, I'm going to faint when you touch me...."

"Yes, so am I," he whispered. He held her eyes. "Look at me."

His fingers moved, and this time they didn't stop. She felt them against the delicate rise of her body, coming down, cupping her in their warmth so that his palm rested gently against the hard tip. And she shuddered, her hands clinging to him, her teeth biting into her lower lip so that she wouldn't cry out.

His hand caressed her tenderly as he held her eyes, and the sound of his fingers against the silky fabric seemed almost as loud as the speaker. "You watched a movie with me when you were about sixteen," he said softly, holding her eyes, "and there was a very adult scene in it where a woman was being seduced. She cried out, and you were concerned that the man was hurting her. Do you remember?"

"You said...that she was crazy with pleasure," she whispered. "And I didn't understand."

"And now you do."

"Yes."

His head bent. "I could live forever on your mouth, Kit...." He kissed her gently and then not gently. And she clung to him, turning so that her body pressed against his and the whole world disappeared as his hand suddenly went under her blouse and against her soft, bare skin.

"It drives me wild when you cry out like

that," he whispered roughly in her ear, his hand contracting as her body arched. "God, touching you like this is so sweet. So sweet." He kissed her trembling lips softly, tenderly, and his fingers stroked her lightly as a breath, lingering at the tiny hardness that told him everything she was feeling.

A sound outside the car brought Matt's head up. He was breathing as unsteadily as she was, and his mouth looked a little swollen, sensuous. He glanced in the rearview mirror and slowly moved his hand to her shoulder with an uneven sigh.

"You'd better sit up, honey," he said quietly. "We're about to have company."

He reached into his pocket for a cigarette and lit it, then slid his arm around a shaking Catherine as he pretended an avid interest in the movie. A strolling policeman with a flashlight wandered by, glancing into the truck and then going on along the row.

Catherine watched as a young couple under a blanket struggled furiously to get separated as the flashlight aimed itself into their car. The policeman stopped there, and she turned her attention back to the screen, thinking how embarrassed she'd have been if he'd come along just a little sooner.

"He's the safety valve," Matt said quietly, smiling down at her. He leaned closer. "Strolling birth control."

She burst out laughing and buried her face in his chest. "You're horrible!"

"You didn't seem to think so a few minutes ago."

She nuzzled closer. "Didn't I?"

His fingers stroked her cheek and he pressed a slow, tender kiss into her disheveled hair. "I guess we'd better watch the movie. I can imagine how the family would react if they had to bail us out of jail for indecent exposure."

"They wouldn't believe it," she said simply.

He looked down at her. "They'd believe it, all right," he said, studying her face. "You look as if you've been made love to."

"So do you," she returned.

He smiled slowly. "I'll have to teach you how," he murmured. "You don't quite know how to give it back yet, do you?"

"I'm just a beginner," she reminded him, trying to keep her head.

"You'll stay that way, too, in the important way," he said, his voice deep and serious as he met her gaze. "Do you understand me, Kit? Seduction is not part of the plan."

"You won't take me to bed?" she asked with mock incredulity. "What's wrong with me?"

"Not one damned thing," he returned. "Except that Betty trusts me." He drew her close and kissed her forehead lightly. "I have to take excellent care of you, Kit. The last thing I want is a shotgun wedding."

That brought it all back. "The last thing you want is a wedding, period," she said, forcing herself to be light about it though she was dying because he didn't want to marry her. "Join the club. I have a career to look forward to, once I convince you that I'm capable of it."

He frowned, as if he hadn't expected her reply. "Are you serious?"

"Of course! You did promise me, Matt," she reminded him, and quickly put her day's work to the back of her mind. She knew he wouldn't keep that promise, and so did he. But when she failed miserably, he'd let her go. He'd probably buy the ticket. And that was a little depressing, especially after what they'd just shared. She cocked her head at him. "You promised," she repeated.

He sighed, turning his eyes back to the screen. "So I did."

She laid her head back against his broad chest, loving him so much that she hurt all over. But she couldn't let him see that. "Sorry."

"About what?"

"That your strategy didn't work," she murmured. "I like kissing you, Matt, but it won't keep me on Comanche Flats."

His face, if she'd seen it, would have been a revelation. His arm tightened around her roughly for a minute before he relaxed and brought his cigarette back to his lips. "Well then, little Kit, I guess I'll have to find another tack."

That was an admission, she told herself. He'd brought her here trying to give her another incentive to stay home. He knew she wanted him, although he didn't know how much. Well, it wouldn't work. She was going to New York, where she wouldn't be vulnerable, and she was going to find a man who'd love her, not dominate her.

"But meanwhile," he murmured, tipping her head back, "I'm going to see to it that you get a little educating in the things that matter. Just so that you can protect yourself." And his mouth went down against hers roughly, hungrily and for so long that she was dazed when he finally lifted it again. He searched her shocked eyes. "Just don't get addicted to me, honey," he added in a cutting tone, "because nobody gets me for keeps. Not even you."

She could hardly believe what she'd heard. Matt had never been cynical with her before. "I won't," she promised curtly.

He laughed mirthlessly. "We'll see."

Her fingers touched his mouth as he started to bend again. "You might warn the real estate agent from Laredo, too," she said, smiling as the shock touched his face. "She might need the warning even more than I do." She turned her attention back to the screen, and he slowly crushed out his cigarette in the ashtray.

"Who told you about Layne?" he asked quietly.

She gave him a haughty stare. "Do you think the family doesn't know about your women, just because you don't bring them home?"

His eyes returned to hers, quiet, watchful. "Layne is working on a project with me," he said after a minute. "I'm expanding a feedlot, and she has a client with land that adjoins mine."

"What does she look like?" she asked, hating herself for wanting to know.

He didn't seem to mind telling her, oddly enough. He even smiled. "She's twenty-nine, tall, dark-eyed and dark-haired."

"And experienced?" she asked.

"And experienced. Most of my women are, if you're curious about that part of my life. You've never expressed any interest in it until now."

"I'm not interested," she hedged.

"No?" He stretched lazily, and her eyes went uncontrollably to the lean, hard-muscled length of his body, down his broad chest to his narrow hips and powerful long legs and big booted feet. "I like your body, too, Kit," he murmured, catching her out. "I especially like the way it feels."

"What an interesting movie!" she enthused, crossing her arms as she curled up on the seat to watch the space creature devour a human.

"Is it? If you won't sit on my lap, then give me your hand." He reached out his lean fingers and laced hers with them. Then he leaned back to smoke another cigarette and watch the movie while Catherine ground her teeth in frustration.

They went home at midnight in a silence unbroken except for the radio. She walked into the house beside Matt, conflicting emotions tearing at her self-control. She didn't know what he wanted, and she was afraid, now that he'd seen how vulnerable she was to him.

Once he'd closed and locked the outside door, she turned, wanting to ask him what the game was. But he turned back and, holding her eyes with his dark ones, he tossed his Stetson onto the hall table. He started toward her with a steady, measured stride.

"Matt..." she began.

He caught her by the waist and drew her to

him. "It's a hell of a lot more exciting to kiss standing up," he murmured. "Come closer, Kit. Your legs won't melt if they touch mine."

"I don't—" She caught her breath as his hands slid to her hips and brought her thighs into total contact with his.

"That's better," he whispered, smiling wickedly.

"Mama told me not to ever—" she tried again.

"Shut up." He bent and caught the back of her head with both hands, holding her face where he wanted it while his mouth made mincemeat of her protests. He forced her set lips to part, and his tongue penetrated the soft line of them delicately, sensually. His hips moved slowly against hers in a rhythm that made her blush, and still the kiss went on and on until it had the effect he meant it to have. With a tiny moan, she stood on tiptoe to get closer to him and linked her arms around his neck to lift herself in an even more intimate embrace.

"Yes," he breathed into her hungry mouth. "Yes!" His arms lifted her clear of the floor, and the world spun away in a blaze of open mouths and wildly beating hearts.

She couldn't get enough of him. It was so sweet to kiss him like this, to feel his heart slamming at the walls of his chest, to feel his teeth cutting into her lip as he deepened and lengthened the hard, devouring kiss.

All at once his body went rigid. Quickly, he put her back on her feet and held her away from him. He looked down at her with dark, smoldering eyes.

"Go upstairs, honey," he said huskily. "Go fast."

"But Matt," she protested, her voice a mere whisper, her body trembling.

"I want you like hell," he ground out, and his desire showed in his eyes, his shaking chest. "Get out of here while you can."

She didn't argue. She wanted to, and for one wild instant she was tempted, but then the logical part of her mind started thinking about consequences, and that sent her up the stairs. She slid her hand along the banister, still tasting Matt on her mouth, her breasts throbbing from the hard pressure of his chest against

them. She stopped at the very top of the stair-
way and looked down.

Matt was standing there, bareheaded, a cigarette in one hand, his eyes intent on her, his
stance rigid.

She lifted her fingers to her lips and impulsively blew him a kiss. And he smiled.

It took all her strength to go on to bed. She
knew suddenly and deliciously that Matt was
as vulnerable as she was. He wanted her. That
gave her a weapon to fight back with, and she
was going to use it. Matt wasn't going to win
this time. She was. At last she could escape
his domination. But did she really want to?

Chapter Five

It was hard to sleep and in the morning it was even harder for Catherine to get on her clothes and go down to breakfast. Everything seemed different. Matt had changed from a wickedly teasing stepcousin into a sensuous stranger. She didn't know how to handle the side of him she'd glimpsed last night, and she couldn't begin to guess at the reason for his behavior. He wasn't looking for permanent ties; he'd made that very plain. Why, then? Just to keep her at home? That didn't seem likely. He wouldn't like her hanging around mooning over him all the time. Maybe he'd had a fight with the real estate agent from Laredo and was just biding his time, playing with her until his ladylove got over her anger.

She still hadn't worked it out when she went downstairs, half excited and half apprehensive about seeing Matt again. She was wearing a green shirtwaist dress with high heels, her hair in a neat French twist, and Matt's eyes came up immediately when he saw her at the doorway of the dining room. She almost jumped at the impact of the level, probing stare, but she didn't look away.

Betty was just finishing her own breakfast. "Good morning, darling," she called gaily. "I'm just off to Jane's for a coffee. That Barnes girl is getting married, you know, and we're all taking turns with the fetes. I'll be back about noon. We can have lunch in town if Matt can spare you."

"I'll do my best," Matt said with a meaningful smile at Catherine. He was looking smart in denim jeans with a chambray shirt open at his chest, and Catherine had to force her eyes away.

"That would be lovely," she told her mother with a bright smile.

Betty kissed her cheek as she passed, neat

in her oyster-colored suit. "See you later. Bye, Matt. Don't the two of you overdo it."

"We won't," he promised, chuckling at Catherine's blush.

She filled her plate, then sat opposite him, ignoring him, vaguely aware of the sound of Betty's car as she drove away.

"I won't go away," he said dryly.

She glanced up as he sipped black coffee. "I should hope not," she said nonchalantly. "You'd break the Laredo real estate agent's heart!"

"How safe is your own, Catherine Melinda?" he asked gently.

Her green eyes searched his. "Safe enough."

"I wonder." He put down his coffee cup. "I want you."

Her eyes widened.

"That's right," he said, reading the shock in her face, "I want you."

"Well, I'm not up for grabs," she began hesitantly.

"I'm going to get you, too," he continued quietly, the threat in his eyes, in his mocking smile. "Run, if you like, and I'll be two steps behind. Until I catch you."

"I'll get pregnant!" she burst out.

His eyebrows shot up. "Not damned likely," he returned. "Not with strolling birth control on patrol."

"I will not go to any more movies with you!" she flashed.

He sighed wearily. "Well, in that case, we're in a lot of trouble. Because if we stay alone together for longer than two minutes, you know as well as I do where it will end."

"Not in your bed," she said firmly.

"It's better on the carpet," he returned outrageously. "More adventurous."

The familiar line made her choke on her coffee. Her wet eyes accused him, but he only grinned.

"I'm going to New York to be a public relations person," she told him.

"Not until you finish my sale, you aren't," he replied easily. He leaned back in his chair, watching her, and slowly flicked open yet another button on his shirt.

Her eyes widened as that broad expanse of deeply tanned skin and thick, curling hair peeked out. She swallowed, dragging her gaze to her plate.

"Do I disturb you, Kit?" he murmured. "I can't imagine why. You've seen me without a shirt before."

Sure she had, and she'd gone wobbling off on weak knees every single time; Matt without a shirt on was enough to have that effect on an eighty-year-old manhater. He was perfect.

"We'll be late getting to the office," she said in a choked tone, then finished her bacon and sipped her coffee.

"I'm the boss, remember?"

She dabbed her lips and got up. "I'll just freshen my makeup—"

"Not yet." He cocked his head and looked her up and down with an expression in his dark eyes that made rubber out of her knees. "Come here."

"Matt…"

"Come here, Kit," he said in a tone that would have tamed a charging elephant.

Her legs rebelled. They took her to him, unresisting.

He reached up and drew her down across his lap, turning her, cradling her. "Put this...here." He took her free hand, the one that wasn't curled around his neck, and slid it into the opening of his shirt, watching her expression as she felt his warm hair-roughened skin.

"Yes, I like that," he whispered, bending to her mouth. "I like it a lot. Stroke me, Kit."

"I hate you," she managed with a shaky breath.

"Sure you do. Open your mouth and kiss me."

She did, her neck arching at the wild, warm hunger of his open lips as they moved hungrily against hers. Her fingers caught in the thick hair over his chest and tugged at it, spearing into its thickness, feeling the hardness of muscle beneath it, the hard pulse of his heartbeat.

"Oh, God," he breathed unsteadily. He moved one hand to rip open the remaining shirt buttons and took her fingers on a journey of discovery right down to the taut, rippling muscles of his stomach.

"Matt." His name sounded like a moan, and her eyes opened, looking up helplessly into his.

"I could make a meal of you, right here,"

he whispered roughly. His hand pressed hers against his chest. "You make the blood rush to my head when you touch me."

She pressed closer, wondering where along the way she'd lost her resolutions. All that seemed to matter now was getting as close to him as she could. His arms wrapped around her, riveting her torso to his, and his face pressed into the curve of her throat and shoulder. He curled her into his lap, rocking her gently against him, while she drowned in his warm strength and the spicy scent of his body.

Where it might have gone from there was anyone's guess, but there was a sudden commotion in the yard as two of the ranch pickups arrived together, apparently in a race. That and their loud voices broke the spell, giving Catherine a chance to collect herself and push out of Matt's enveloping arms.

She got a little distance away and made an effort to reorganize her wild hair and mind, her breath coming all too quickly. She had to stop letting him do that. It was her own fault. The problem was that he was playing and she wasn't.

With her pride carefully in hand, she shot a

glance at him as she pushed back the loosened strands of hair. "What's the matter, aren't you getting what you need from the lady in Laredo, Matt?" she asked as carefully as she could, when inside her blood was rippling like white water. "Or am I just a novelty?"

That seemed to take him by surprise. He cocked his head at her, his dark Spanish eyes piercing and level. "Why don't you work on that for a few days, honey, and tell me what you come up with?" He actually grinned at her as he buttoned his shirt and smoothed his own hair. "You'd better do something about your hair," he added. "And a little lipstick might help that pretty, swollen mouth. God, it's sweet to kiss!"

She didn't know whether to laugh or cry or scream. She stared at him with her mind whirling, her body throbbing.

He stood up. "Don't look so worried, Kit, it's all pretty simple. But I keep forgetting how young you are."

"I'm old enough to know that you're one of those men Mama's spent the past six years telling me about," she returned.

He lifted a cigarette to his curving lips and lit it. "Am I?"

"I won't have an affair with you," she told him bluntly, her green eyes throwing off sparks.

His eyebrows jackknifed. "My God, how would we manage that around here?" he asked. "This place is worse than Grand Central Station! Hal's forever playing tricks, sticking his nose in. Annie's as bad. And your mother, God love her, is as curious as she is the image of you! We'd have to conduct it under the house and even then, Hal would drill holes in the floor to get a better view!"

She tried not to laugh, but her eyes gave her away.

"An affair," he scoffed. His eyes went up and down her. He pursed his lips in mock thoughtfulness. "Although, maybe if we got in the truck and painted the windows black and locked it from the inside—"

"Matt!" she said sharply, her eyes glowering.

"Oh, well, I'll work on it, Kit, You just give me some time." He chuckled, ignoring the fury in her eyes. "Go fix your face. I've got a cattleman coming to look over some culls."

With a sigh, she turned and went toward the stairs. Trying to talk to Matt was like trying to talk to a wall, and about as satisfying. She didn't know any more about his intentions now than she had last night. The only thing she knew for sure was how vulnerable she was. She'd have to keep out of his way from now on or grow a shell. Matt, in pursuit, was formidable.

He seemed to sense her unease, her wariness, because when she came back downstairs, he slipped back into the old, familiar camaraderie and kept it up all the way to the office. She was visibly relaxed by the time they started work.

"Having any trouble with that?" he asked, gesturing toward the computer.

She remembered the crashed program disk and hoped Angel wouldn't give her away. "No," she said airily. "Of course not."

"Then why are you using a backup program disk?" he asked casually, lifting the backup diskette in a lean, tanned hand.

She swallowed. "Why not?"

He chuckled and handed it back. "Everybody crashes a disk now and again. Don't sweat it. How's the listing coming? Got a printout yet?"

How would he react, she wondered, if she showed him her listing of his award-winning cattle? Debutante heifers... She cleared her throat. "Actually," she began, "I'd really rather not worry you with it just yet. I have some more work to do before it's ready."

"Okay," he said easily. "Just don't take too long, honey. It needs to be at the printer's next Monday morning."

"Oh, I'll have it by then, don't worry."

"Angel has last year's booklet. That might help."

"I've already asked her for it," she replied, one jump ahead of him. Her eyes involuntarily dropped to his hard mouth, and she couldn't help the way she stared at it with remembered pleasure.

"Not now," he murmured softly, wickedly. "I have to keep my mind on my work."

He sauntered off before she could manage a sharp comeback.

While he was with his visiting cattleman,

she drew out the file of cattle he was selling off and quietly changed it so that it read as it should. She was going to give up the idea of sabotaging his sale. After all, if she wanted to get to New York, her best bet, she decided, was to prove her worth as a public relations expert and then make Matt keep his promise. Fouling up things would only prolong the agony. And if he was going to start pursuing her, she'd have to work fast. She knew she'd never be able to hold out against him.

Angel poked her head around the door just before noon. "Want to come out with Gail and Dorothy and me for a sandwich?" she asked with a smile.

"I'd love to, but I promised to have lunch with my mother," Catherine said apologetically. "Another time?"

"Fine! If you want to run along now, I'll lock up. Matt went out with Mr. Landers for a business lunch, so he won't be back until afternoon."

"Okay, I'll just close down here." Catherine took out the disk and turned off the machine.

It wasn't until she was on her way to town

with Betty that she remembered she hadn't stored the changed information on the disk. She'd cut off the machine with all the changes still in limbo.

"Oh, no," she groaned. "Now I'll have to do it all over again!"

"Do what, darling?" Betty asked.

"Never mind," Catherine sighed, shaking her head. "Just something else I've fouled up. Oh well, it will all come right in the end, I guess."

The rest of the way into town Betty kept the conversation going all alone. And after they sat down to eat she noticed that Catherine sat and played with her food and did little more than nibble.

Catherine's mind was awash with new images of Matt, with feelings she didn't know how to handle, with longings that made her young body burn. She hadn't felt these sensations before. They were alien and sweet and heady. And she was sure that Matt was only playing, that he wasn't serious. How could he be, when everyone knew he was a confirmed bachelor? Besides, there was the real estate agent from Laredo. Layne. Catherine grimaced at the picture Matt had conjured by talking about the woman. "Experienced," he'd said. Sure. And probably even more experienced by now, after sleeping with Matt. Her eyes closed. She couldn't bear to think of him with another woman. It had hurt for years when he went on dates, but having experienced his ardor for herself, it was so much worse. From now on, she'd be able to picture exactly what he was doing, and it would pierce her heart every time. How would she bear it? She had to get away. And what if the mysterious Layne got through his defenses and he married her? Tears stung her eyes, shocking her.

"I said, how is it going at the office, Catherine?" Betty prodded. Then she saw the distress on her daughter's face and she frowned. "Darling, what's wrong?"

"I crashed a system disk," she blurted out.

"Oh. Well, I don't suppose Matt will yell too much," she comforted her daughter, patting her hand gently. "Don't worry about it."

It wasn't that, but even as she stared hopefully at her mother, she knew she couldn't share her problem. Betty was a loving mother, but she couldn't keep secrets. She'd blurt it out to someone, probably Annie, who'd tell everyone else. That would make it much worse. The only person Catherine had ever been able to tell secrets to was Matt, who was a clam. But she couldn't very well tell Matt she was in love with him.

Catherine finished her coffee and gave a wistful sigh. Well, she'd get through somehow.

The other girls were already hard at work when Catherine arrived back at the office. Angel gestured toward Matt's closed office door and looked toward the ceiling, a warning if ever there was one. Catherine nodded conspiratorially and eased his door open, then sneaked to her own desk just as a tight, very controlled burst of blue language colored the air around Matt.

He glanced at Catherine, the pencil between his fingers bouncing up and down against the desk as he listened and nodded.

"All right. Meet me at the airport in an hour. I'll talk to him. Sure. Bye, honey."

He hung up, and Catherine made a production of booting up her computer and inserting the program disk.

"I have to fly to Dallas," he said abruptly, rising. "There's been a hitch in the deal for that ranch property I'm trying to buy. Layne said the landowner is trying to jack up the price."

Her pulse leaped as he came to stand beside her. "I thought your real estate agent was from Laredo," she said, trying to sound calm though her pulse was all over the place.

"She was born there, but she lives in Dallas," he said, clearing up the mystery. He stared down at her. "Hal's due back today."

"Is he? How nice."

"I don't want you going out with him."

That brought her head up. She stared at him uncomprehendingly. "What?"

"You heard me." He wasn't teasing now. His gaze was dark and unblinking, his face hard. He was the stranger again, not the familiar jovial man she thought she knew.

"But—"

He reached down, caught her by the upper arms and drew her slowly but relentlessly to her feet so that she was all too close to his powerful, hard-muscled body. His breath was warm and spicy just above her mouth, his eyes watchful, strange.

"Hal competes with me. He always has. If he thinks I want something, he'll do his damndest to beat me out of it."

"But, I don't even feel that way about Hal," she began hesitantly. He was making her feel the wildest hungers. Her hands pressed against his shirt and felt the hard beat of his heart. "And anyway, what...what business is it of yours if I...?" Suddenly her voice faltered.

"You're trembling, Kit," he whispered, his mouth against her lips. His fingers trailed along her throat, inciting, wildly sensuous as he bent his head. "And I can make it even worse."

He did. His mouth covered hers, exploring every soft inch of it with his tongue, biting tenderly at the curve of her upper lip, and all the while his hands smoothed her body to his, so that she could feel the warm muscle, the strength of him. Her hands clutched at his shirt as if she were drowning.

His hands slid down to her hips as he brought her close enough to feel how aroused

he was. She protested, but he held her there
and lifted his head to stare into her turbulent
eyes.

"It's all right," he whispered. "Think of it
as nonverbal communication."

Her breath was coming in soft gasps; it disturbed her to know how hungry he was for
her. It was new, just as everything with him
seemed to be.

"Such big eyes," he murmured, smiling.

"I've never...been like this with a man before," she confessed.

His hands came up to smooth back loose
wisps of her hair, but she didn't try to move
away. She felt a sudden tremor in his powerful, jeans-clad legs, and her eyes asked a question.

"I'd like to lie with you, Kit," he whispered, then searched her eyes in the hot silence
that followed. His eyes slid sideways to the
sofa and back again, and his jaw clenched as
his breath came roughly. "I'd like to strip you
down to the waist and put my mouth... here."
One lean hand moved between them. His
knuckles drew lightly up and down over the
very tip of her breast. He felt it harden, and

heard the shocked surge of her breath as it caught.

"Matt," she moaned. Her eyes held his; she was beyond thought, beyond reason. Her body tingled, and she wanted him to see her, to pull off her blouse and look at her as no other man ever had.

"Yes, you'd let me, wouldn't you?" he breathed, looking down at her yielded body, where his fingers now gently searched one perfect, high breast. His thumb rubbed slowly over the throbbing tip and she bit her lip to keep from crying out, her body stiffening, shuddering with unexpected pleasure.

His eyes searched her face, seeing and appreciating the helpless reaction there. "Oh, Kit," he breathed. "What a hell of a time to go all-woman on me. Here I am with a plane to catch and all I want to do is back you up against the wall and crush your body with mine and make your mouth swell with my kisses."

Her lips parted spontaneously at the imagery. "The...wall?" she whispered shakily.

She saw the flash of his eyes, felt herself shudder. He moved, backing her past the sofa, holding her eyes, until they reached the bare wall beside the door.

"Yes. The wall." His body arched down, and he held her eyes as his hips and thighs flattened hers in an intimacy that widened her eyes, opened her mouth, that made her body burn and throb and shudder with frank desire.

The pleasure was almost pain. She made a wild little sound under her breath and felt it go into his open mouth as he bent to her trembling lips and took them. It was an incredible kind of kiss, without pressure, without tangible hunger. It was so tender that she tasted the moist brush of his lips and could feel their very texture, could feel them tremble with the most terrible longing. His eyes were open, and so were hers, and they watched each other in a burning silence as his hips moved suggestively, tenderly, against hers. She felt the wildest kind of ache, and in the throes of it, her hips began to rotate sharply against his, and she moaned, pleading with her eyes as her nails bit into him. She felt him go rigid, heard the rough groan, and she stopped the hungry motion abruptly, apparently just in time.

"What sweet agony that was, Kit," he

whispered shakily near her mouth. "And if you move that way again, I'll take you standing up."

She stood quite still, reading the truth in his dark, hot eyes, in the sudden bruising grip of his fingers as they found her hips. And she knew that the slightest movement on her part would cost him his self-control.

He took slow, harsh breaths until he got back the control he'd lost, until he finally collapsed against her, his face at her throat, his body shuddering with the effort.

"Matt," she whispered at his ear. Her arms were around his neck, though she had no idea how they'd got there. She could hear the thunder of his pulse, the rasp of his painful breathing. She didn't move a muscle because Betty had once told her how it was for a man. And this was her fault because she'd forgotten. "Matt, I'm sorry."

"Oh, baby, you burn me up," he whispered roughly. "You make me so damned hungry. Kit, that was a near thing."

She blushed and clung closer, nuzzling against his warm throat. "Are you all right?"

"I'd be a hell of a lot better if we didn't

have so many clothes on," he said, nibbling at her ear. "I'd like to feel your skin touching mine, all the way up and down, little virgin."

Her nails bit into him, and she pressed her face closer in an agony of longing.

"Don't," he whispered. His hands bit into her back, pulling her away from the wall even as he put some little distance between her legs and his.

"Then stop making me feel this way," she whisered back. "You do it with words."

"Verbal lovemaking," he breathed into her ear. "I could make you give yourself to me without ever touching you. I could describe it to you...every single detail...."

"No," she moaned. She pulled back, and he bent, catching her mouth with his.

He lifted her in a bruising embrace, and she gave him back the kiss without the slightest protest, her arms clinging, her mouth opening sweetly to the probing demand of his. Somewhere in the distance a phone was ringing, voices murmured, the wind blew. And all she knew was the scent and feel of Matt.

A long minute later, he let her slide back to her feet and lifted his dark head. The look in his eyes surprised her a little because it was so blatantly possessive.

"You're going to be my woman," he said under his breath, staring into her dazed eyes. "Remember that when Hal comes home."

He let her go abruptly and watched her grab the back of a chair for support.

He laughed mockingly, dragging a cigarette from his pocket with fingers that were slightly unsteady. "Can't you stand, Kit? I feel trembly myself. My Lord, you're sweet to make love to!"

She could hardly find enough breath to answer him. "What do you want from me?"

"Lots of things," he murmured, letting his eyes wander down her soft, slender body.

"Things you can't get from Layne?" she asked angrily.

He pursed his lips and studied her. "Layne isn't a virgin," he said.

Her face flamed with anger and embarrassment. She glared at him over the back of the chair. "How sad for you," she burst out. "Just don't think I'm going to take her place."

"That would be difficult," he agreed. He

grinned at her. "Speaking of Layne, I'd better get moving. She's expecting me."

"By all means, don't let me hold you up."

"You look as if someone needs to," he observed, moving toward the door. "Want me to pour you a brandy before I go, honey?" he added wickedly.

"You were the one who needed fortifying a minute ago," she returned with an odd sense of pride.

"So I was." He lifted the cigarette to his mouth and watched her through slitted eyes. "We'd have to make love on asbestos sheets, Kit, or we'd set fires."

She picked up a book from his desk and prepared to heave it at him, but he was out the door, laughing, before she could lift it over her head.

Chapter Six

Hal showed up about supper time, all smiles. Matt had phoned the office just before quitting time to have Angel relay the message that he was going to be in Dallas for several days. That information had made Catherine see red; she was sure he was spending more time with the mysterious Layne than he was on business.

She'd come home in a flap and hadn't come out of it until Hal breezed in the door, bearing a bouquet of exquisite daisies and mums and baby's breath.

"For you," he said with a grin. "There's a flower shop at the airport. I couldn't resist them."

"Oh, Hal, how beautiful!" She lifted the bouquet to her nose, inhaling its beautiful fragrance. "You're a nice man."

He grinned at her with a smile that was too much like Matt's. "My pleasure. Where's old steely eyes?"

"If you mean Matt, dear, he's in Dallas," Betty volunteered as she gestured them into the dining room, where Annie was putting dishes of food on the set table. "He won't be back for several days, didn't he say, Catherine?"

"That's right," she agreed tightly, letting Hal seat her across from Betty. "Several days."

"Aha." Hal glanced speculatively at Catherine before he turned and sat down. "The lovely Layne again, no doubt," he added with soft malice, pinning Catherine with his eyes as he said it, seeing the flicker of her eyelids. "Have you heard about her?"

"Angel said she calls him a lot."

"That isn't all she does," Hal murmured. "From what I hear, she has a way with men."

"Have you met her?" Catherine had to know.

"You know how possessive Matt is about his women, sweet," he said nonchalantly. "He doesn't like competition, so I've never been introduced."

"As if you could compete with Matt, darling," Betty teased.

Hal's face hardened, but he didn't fire back. He helped himself to smothered steak and held out his cup for Annie to fill with freshly brewed black coffee.

"They don't usually last long," Catherine pointed out. She toyed with her carrots. "Matt's women," she emphasized.

"Layne's been around for some time," Hal told her. He savored a piece of steak. "She has staying power, I suppose. You know how determined those successful real estate agents are. They keep going until they get what they want." He lifted his coffee cup and pointedly glanced over the rim at Catherine. "He sent her a barrel of roses on her birthday. I saw the bill. I could have lived on that amount for a month, even the way I spend money."

Catherine felt her body going taut. So she'd been right about Layne and right about Matt's lack of commitment. He'd only been playing with her. She was something to fill in the time when he wasn't with Layne. Well, two could play that game.

"How about riding over to Fort Worth with me tomorrow?" Hal asked her. "I have to see a man about a sports car I'm thinking of buying."

"I'd love to," Catherine said shortly.

"But, darling, don't you have to work on Matt's sale?" Betty asked, her voice hesitant.

"I'm entitled to a few hours off," Catherine replied. "I'll get it done in time, don't worry. What time do you want to leave?" she asked Hal.

He smiled coolly. "About nine. We'll make a day of it."

"I'll look forward to it," Catherine assured him.

Betty lingered over her dessert, shooting worried glances at Catherine until Catherine couldn't take it any longer and went up to bed.

Fort Worth was big and sprawling, and Catherine loved the variety of shops it offered, but Hal was far more interested in seeing his sports car than in watching his cousin shop for clothes.

"We'll stop by one of the malls on the way back if we have time," he said, placating her.

She didn't argue. After all, it was his trip, not hers. She leaned back with a sigh in the seat of his Ferrari. "Why do you want a new one?" she asked curiously, savoring the leather luxury of the year-old automobile.

"Are you kidding? It's last year's," he said, as if she were asking why he wanted to trade in a moth-eaten suit. "I travel first class, kid."

She studied him quietly as he drove, comparing him with Matt. Matt never minded driving one of the pickup trucks. He kept the Lincoln for business, but she'd seen him borrow a friend's Volkswagen and rave about it to the owner. Matt didn't have his head in the clouds. He was a down-to-earth man with no illusions about being better because he had money. Of course, there was this problem he had with women....

She shifted restlessly. "Are you going to get another Ferrari?" she asked conversationally.

"Sure. Why not?" He grinned.

She sighed. "Well, it's sure beyond my pocket," she said with a smile. "I'm lucky to be able to afford a VW, especially since Matt's cut off my allowance.'' She'd so allowed herself to be charmed by Matt that she'd forgotten that villainous action, but she wasn't admitting that to Hal. How desperately she'd been charmed was something she wanted only to forget!

Hal glanced at her as he took a corner on two wheels. ''It's beyond my pocket, too, honey, but as long as I've got brother Matt to cosign, I can buy anything I like.''

''Matt's cosigning with you?'' she gasped.

''Not exactly,'' he admitted. ''But what he doesn't know won't hurt him.'' His face darkened and he scowled. ''God knows, I never get anything unless I fight him. I get tired of begging for what's mine.''

She could feel his bitterness, but she kept thinking about how hard Matt had worked to build up the family's holdings to make it possible for Hal to buy expensive sports cars. Matt hardly ever took any time off, and Hal never did anything except spend. It seemed a little one-sided to her.

She almost said so, but she curbed her temper. After all, Matt wasn't in her good graces at the moment, either. He was off with his Layne, probably having a ball.

"Why don't you take a job with the company, Hal?" she asked gently. "It's what Matt really wants. That's why he makes it so hard for you."

"I don't want a job with the company, Catherine," Hal muttered. He pushed the accelerator a little harder as they sped out onto the highway. "I want to race cars. It's all I've ever wanted, but I can't make Matt understand that I'm not cut out to be a minor executive."

"Have you tried talking to him?" she persisted.

"Talk to Matt?" he burst out, taking his eyes off the road to fix her with an astonished stare. "When did he ever listen? He just turns around and walks off. You know how he is."

"Why don't you turn around and follow him?"

"Because the last time I did that, he hauled back and slugged me," he grumbled. "Nobody could ever accuse big brother of being a wimp; that's for sure."

"You could leave home, Hal, and do it on your own," she reminded him.

"That's a laugh," he told her flatly, and pushed the sports car even harder. "How could I get a job driving without the money to buy my way in?"

"Other people manage."

"I'm not other people," he replied. He took a sharp curve without slowing at all, the tires screeching wildly. "And I'm not giving up my inheritance, not even to get one-up on Matt."

"Hal, hadn't you better slow down?" she asked, apprehension in her voice as she tried to hang on to the dash. And as she spoke, from behind them came the sound of a siren. She turned in the seat to find a state patrol car in hot pursuit. "Oh, Lord!" she cried. "Now we're in for it."

Hal let out a word she rarely heard, and glared in the rearview mirror. "Just my luck," he muttered. "I might just be able to outrun them...."

Before she could react, he'd stomped down on the accelerator. "Hal, no!" she cried, but he wasn't listening.

"If they catch me speeding and Matt hears about it, I'll never get my new car," he said sharply. "So they aren't catching me. Hold on, honey!"

Hal was hopeless. Like the other members of the family, she wondered sometimes if he would ever grow up. She grabbed the dash and held on for dear life as Hal turned the car in the middle of the superhighway and sped back the other way, passing the state patrol car.

Catherine had never before been so afraid. She knew Hal had a wild streak, and she'd voluntarily gone with him. Matt would kill them both, starting with his brother. Inevitably, the police would get him. Hadn't Hal learned that much?

The car careened wildly as Hal crossed center lines, passed on blind curves, and took corners on two wheels. There were two patrol cars in pursuit now, and Catherine knew there would be others farther down the road. Hal had to be crazy! The patrol car was so close behind that they'd have the tag number by now. With a quick check they'd know Hal owned it. They'd have his name and address, and would only have to come to the house and arrest him.

She half turned in the seat to tell Hal so, just as his face froze, and his eyes widened.

"Oh, damm!" he burst out.

A trouble light had suddenly popped into view and Hal hit the wheel to avoid the hole in the road under the light. The car barreled across the shoulder and down an embankment, then came to a sudden, sickening stop against a telephone pole, the sound of shattering glass and ripping metal loud in Catherine's ears.

If they hadn't been wearing seat belts, something Catherine had been angrily persistent about, they'd have been killed. As it was, Hal's nose had hit the steering wheel and was bleeding profusely.

Catherine was all right, except for a wrist that had been wrenched when she'd frantically braced herself against the dash.

"You okay?" Hal asked her quickly as he reached for a handkerchief to hold against his nose.

"I think so," she said falteringly.

Suddenly sirens were everywhere. Tires screeched. A door opened and closed angrily, and then a uniformed state trooper looked in through the open top and sighed as he surveyed the two occupants.

"You're both damned lucky," he told Hal. "If you'd rolled it, no power on earth would have saved you. Can you walk?"

"Sure," Hal said, dabbing at his nose with the handkerchief.

"Are you all right, miss?" the officer asked, studying Catherine, whose face was as white as cornmeal.

"I think so," she said in a ghostly tone. She grimaced as she moved her hand. "Except for my wrist. I must have...have wrenched it."

"Sit tight," the officer advised gently. "There'll be an ambulance along in a minute or two; the E.M.T.s will know what to do."

She nodded and leaned back in the seat, grateful to be alive. And while Hal went along with the uniformed officer to answer some pointed questions, Catherine wondered how Hal was going to explain his way out of this one. Matt would be a wild man when he found out. Especially when he found out that she had been with Hal, because Matt had told her not to go off with his brother.

Well, she excused herself, he'd gone off

with Layne, hadn't he? What right did he have
to dictate to her? And then she looked at the
mess she was in and decided that maybe, just
maybe, he'd been right to forbid her Hal's
company. Hal was definitely not the ideal driving companion.

They were taken to the nearest hospital,
where Catherine's wrist was bandaged. Only
bruised, they told her, and fortunately the sore-
ness would soon be gone.

Hal was scratched, and his nose had taken
a beating, but he was fine. At least, he was
fine until he had to call Betty to ask her to find
a bail bondsman. He'd been arrested on five
counts of reckless driving and faced several
days in jail unless someone posted bail.

Catherine didn't even feel sorry for him. As
they were driven to police headquarters, he
was still raving about his monumental bad
luck and wasn't showing a shred of guilt for
what he'd done. Through her anger, Catherine
wondered vaguely why Matt didn't let Hal do
what he really wanted to—race cars. That had
been the dream of Hal's life, but Matt never
listened. He talked only about the company.
That was to be Hal's future.

Betty arrived an hour later, nervous and un-
easy. She turned over documents and spoke to
the police sergeant at the desk while Catherine
sat nervously and quietly on a bench in the
waiting area along with a scattering of drunks
and prostitutes who were waiting to be
booked. Minutes later, Catherine and Hal were
released, and Betty took them home.

"Those people." Betty shuddered as she
drove. "How terrible to have to wait alone in
a place like that," she murmured, glancing at
Catherine in the front seat beside her. "Darling, I'm so sorry!"

"It was all right. I was too numb to notice,"
Catherine replied. She glanced in the back
seat. Hal was sound asleep!

"Is he awake?" Betty asked softly.

"He's snoring." Catherine laughed mirthlessly. "Oh, Lord, Matt will kill us both!"

"No doubt. And I'm afraid he'll be at the
house by the time I get back with you two,"
Betty added grimly. "He called seconds after
you hung up. I had to tell him."

Catherine felt her face going bloodless. "He
was coming home?"

"He said he'd meet us at the house." Betty

peered ahead into the darkness. "Why did Hal do it?" she moaned.

"He was afraid of a speeding ticket," Catherine answered.

"So he tried for a few reckless-driving charges instead."

"That's about the size of it." It was getting dark quickly. Feeling limp with relief that it was finally over, Catherine closed her eyes. "I hope his life insurance is paid up." The thought of facing Matt didn't relax her one bit. She could picture his face in her mind.

And when they got home, his face looked exactly as she'd imagined it. He was pacing the porch with a lit cigarette in his hand, waiting.

Matt whirled as they came slowly up the steps, his black eyes riveted on Catherine as if she were a ghost.

"Are you all right?" he asked immediately, his gaze missing nothing as it flashed over her. He was frozen in place now, motionless. Catherine noticed he was still wearing his suit slacks and dress shirt, although he'd long since removed the tie and jacket.

"Just a sore wrist," she told him. She stood

beside Hal, feeling dragged out, and wondered at the emotion in Matt's hard face as he faced his brother.

"And you?" he asked Hal curtly.

"I'll live," Hal said coldly. "Just my damned luck to get busted when I was on my way to trade cars."

"You could have killed Catherine and yourself," Matt said; the look in his eyes would have melted steel.

Hal shrugged. "I guess so. I didn't expect them to catch us."

"How many times do I have to tell you that the highway isn't a racetrack?" Matt shot at him, his voice deepening in anger.

"Then why the hell won't you let me get off the highways and onto a racetrack?" Hal returned. "I have every right in the world to do what I want with my own life!"

"And when you inherit the trust, you can," Matt agreed. "But until then, I'll do what I promised Mother, and that means you're going to learn the real estate business. Whether or not it kills us both."

"Mother's dead, Matt!"

For an instant, he only stared at Hal. Then,

dismissing him, he turned to Catherine, letting his dark eyes reveal his concern. "What about that wrist?"

Hal muttered something and went inside, slamming the door furiously behind him.

"My wrist is all right," Catherine said. She looked up at Matt, and found him closer than she'd expected. "Why won't you let him go?" she added gently. "He's right, you know. He'll never be a company man."

"You, too?" he growled. "For God's sake, this is none of your business!"

That wasn't the familiar Matt. It was the stranger again, the cold, hard man who seemed to turn up at the most unexpected times. She stared at him quietly, trying to comprehend the change.

"You're like your father, aren't you?" she asked absently. "There's the wrong way and your way and no in-between. Can't you see what you're doing to Hal?"

"I'm trying to make a man of him," he replied, lifting the cigarette to his mouth. "Despite interference from you."

"Hal's my friend," she said. "And your

brother. If you wouldn't push him so hard, Matt..."

"I was pushed hard," he reminded her. "It didn't hurt me."

"Didn't it?" She studied his hard features, his dark eyes. "You were raised in a military fashion, with rules and regulations instead of pampering. You never knew tenderness because your mother, in her way, was as hard as your father. But it was different for Hal."

"Yes." He laughed coldly. "He had an adoring stepfather, didn't he?" He finished the cigarette and tossed it off the porch. "He and Jerry."

"You were almost a grown man when your mother remarried," she began gently.

"Thank God. I didn't have to endure watching her fawn over him."

She'd never realized how it must have been for Matt, who worshipped his father. She stared up at him with understanding shining like a beacon in her green eyes. No, Matt had never been loved. But she could love him, if only he'd let her. If he'd just forget Layne....

The memory moved her eyes down to his unbuttoned shirt, to hair-roughened olive skin that looked even darker against the white cotton fabric. Layne.

"I thought you had to spend several days in Dallas," she said then.

"I did. I do. But after I spoke to Betty, I flew straight here. I wanted to make sure Hal hadn't killed you."

Bitterness in his voice, and anger. Her eyes glanced off his. "Well, he hasn't. Won't Layne be lonely?" she added sharply.

"Maybe I'm lonely, too," he said deeply, and smiled mockingly as her head came up and her wide eyes were caught and held by his. "That shocks you, does it, Catherine?" he continued, watching her.

"You aren't my idea of a lonely man," she countered.

"I have the occasional woman," he agreed blatantly. "But I don't spend my life in bed, Kit. There's more to a relationship than just sex."

Of all the things she might have expected him to say, that was the very last. "What with the variety you keep around you, I could be forgiven for doubting you," she replied.

"You don't sleep around," he murmured softly.

"Maybe I do, and I'm just putting on an act for you," she returned hotly, hating the vulnerability he was making her feel.

His chiseled lips drew up in a mocking smile. "Are you?" He moved a step closer. "There's an easy way to find out, Kit," he said in a voice like velvet. "Suppose I asked you to prove it to me?"

"I won't sleep with you!" She backed away, glaring.

"I haven't asked you," he reminded her. "Nervous, Kit? All shaky with anticipation? I could make you go down on your knees and beg, and you know it."

"I am not fair game for your misplaced hunting instincts," she shot at him. "Kindly save your amorous exhibitions for the real estate agent from Laredo!"

"Amorous exhibitions?" he mimicked, his eyebrows arching. "My, my, aren't we verbose tonight. Are you sure it was your wrist you sprained, and not your tongue, honey?"

"There is nothing wrong with my tongue," she returned.

"Not when you put it in the right place," he agreed in a voice that melted her knees and brought back vivid memories of his own tongue tangling with hers.

"I want to go to bed," she blurted out.

"So do I, baby," he murmured, his dark eyes wandering hungrily over her body. "Eager little thing, aren't you, Kit?"

"Damn it, Matt!"

"There, there; you'll blow a fuse," he teased. She started to turn, but catching her by the waist, he moved her right up against his warm, muscular body. He smelled of cologne and soap, and the smell drugged her, making her vulnerable. His steely fingers bit into her waist, holding her. "How's it going at work?" he asked, his lips close to her forehead.

"Everything's...fine."

"Good. I have to fly back to Dallas tonight, and I won't be home again for three days or so. Stay out of Hal's way until I come back," he added firmly. "No more adventures."

She wasn't going off with Hal again anyway, but she didn't like his commanding tone. "I'm an adult now. I can do what I please."

"Now, where have I heard that before?" he asked dryly.

"Matt...!"

His hand tangled in her hair and held her face up to his. "When I get back," he whispered with his mouth poised over hers, "I'm going to make wild, passionate love to you, Kit. I'm going to throw you down on a bed and strip you to the waist and teach you how to make soft, sweet little noises in my ear."

Her heart went crazy. She stared up at him, heart lodged in her throat, eyes hungry, body feverish.

Suddenly he bent her backward—her hair reached toward the floor—and with a wicked, mischievous laugh, made her wait for the slow, lazy descent of his mouth. Held in that off-balance position, she was all too aware of his strength, of his masculinity. His mouth opened her lips, felt them tremble and part; he felt her body go soft, her arms go around him. And he laughed deep in his throat and teased her lips until she moaned.

Then he straightened, bringing her with him, and let her try to reach him, let her stand on tiptoe, trying to find his mouth.

"Oh, no," he whispered with a soft laugh. "Not tonight." He held her arms down by her sides and brushed a lazy kiss against her cheek. "Go to bed, Kit, and dream of me."

"I won't!" she whispered huskily, her eyes accusing as she drew away from him, frustrated and embarrassed.

"You will." He pulled another cigarette from his pocket. "Maybe I'll dream about you, too."

"With Layne in tow? Fat chance!" She whirled and started inside.

"Kit."

She turned and glared at him, her face red. "What?"

"I might be as vulnerable as you are; did you ever consider that?" he asked quietly.

She tried to speak, failed, and quickly went into the house before she could be frightened by the implications of what he was saying. He was just playing, she reminded herself. Just killing time, amusing himself. And afterward he'd go running back to Layne, who was older and sophisticated and fit into his world. And if she had any sense at all, she'd remember that.

Chapter Seven

Matt left later that evening. Hal didn't say another word to his brother. He went to bed early and didn't show his face the whole of the next day.

"He worries me," Betty sighed the following day as she finished her lunch and poured a second cup of coffee for Catherine, who was taking her lunch hour at home instead of going out with the office girls.

"Who?"

"Hal," her mother replied. "He isn't himself lately."

"He's just miserable, that's all," Catherine told her. "He isn't happy with what Matt's making him do."

"Poor Hal. I'm sorry for him, but nobody wins against Matt. I just hope Hal doesn't go back to his old ways and start trying to get back at Matt. He used to pull some of the most horrible tricks. Oh, well, maybe I'm worrying for nothing." She smiled at Catherine. "How's it going at the office?"

"Very well," the younger woman replied, smiling back. "I've just gotten the programs compiled. I let Angel check them to make sure I hadn't done anything unforgivable. Now I'm going to get some ads ready for the newspapers, and some radio spots, and I'm going to compose a letter to send to selected buyers. Then I have to organize a barbecue...."

"It sounds so complicated!" Betty said.

"It is. But it will prove to Matt that I'm capable of making my own way," she replied. "That's something Hal and I have in common, I suppose. We're both trapped here by Matt."

"For vastly different reasons, I imagine," Betty said enigmatically.

"I doubt that." Catherine put down her coffee cup. "I hate to, but I have to get back to work. I want to take a minute and call the public realations agency in New York to see if they'll wait another month for me. It will take at least that long to get this show on the road.''

''Do you think they'll wait to fill the vacancy?'' Betty asked.

Catherine shrugged. ''I don't know. I hope so,'' she said wistfully. ''But you know how Matt is when he digs in his heels. I have to prove myself to him.''

''Maybe he's just trying to make sure you know what you're doing. He doesn't think you'd be happy in New York.''

''Well, I'll never find out from here, will I?'' came the exasperated reply. ''Honestly, sometimes I think Matt just has an overdeveloped sense of responsibility. But he's got to let go sometime!''

''Yes. I suppose so.'' But Betty didn't sound enthusiastic herself.

''I'll write you,'' her daughter coaxed. ''And phone you. I'll come home on holidays.''

''It won't be the same. And who'll make

Matt smile? He never does except for you. When you're away, he's a different man.''

That puzzled Catherine. She'd wondered for a long time about the stranger who appeared from time to time, the hard-faced man with the cold eyes. That wasn't her Matt.

''Have to run, darling,'' she told her mother. ''My computer awaits without.''

''Without what?'' Hal asked from the doorway, all eyes.

''Without a program, that's without what,'' Catherine teased. ''Feeling better?''

''Not really, but it's stifling up there alone. What's to eat?''

''Egg salad, dear,'' Betty said, offering him the plate of sandwiches.

''My favorite.'' He glanced at Catherine in her neat blue suit. ''Who are you dressed up for?''

''The other girls,'' she offered. ''They all dress this way. Sort of office custom.''

''Yes, I've seen Angel.'' He sighed. ''Nice-looking lady.''

Her eyes sharpened. ''Do you think so?''

''Don't get ideas,'' he said curtly. ''I just like the way she looks, that's all.''

"I didn't say a word!"

Betty excused herself to get some coffee, and Hal put his sandwich on his plate and looked at Catherine.

"Does Matt make a habit of kissing you like he did night before last?" he asked abruptly, then nodded at her shocked expression. "Yes, I saw. I was on my way back out to make a stand and got the wind knocked out of my sails. Is he trying to put the make on you, Catherine?"

She had to fight for the right words. "He was only teasing."

"It didn't look like teasing to me."

"Well, it was. So don't start any duels on my behalf. And don't worry Mama with it, either!" she continued, nervous now because of the way he was watching her.

"Oh, I wouldn't do that," he agreed.

He looked smug all at once, and she stared at him curiously.

"Isn't it a beautiful day?" he asked merrily. "I feel much better already. Hadn't you better get to work?"

"Yes, I suppose so," she said absently. "Goodbye, Mama!" she called.

"Goodbye, dear," Betty said with a smile as she rejoined Hal. "Have a nice day."

"Of course," Catherine answered, but there was something about Hal's attitude that made the words into a lie. She didn't like having Hal know that Matt had kissed her. He might find a way to turn the knowledge into a weapon in his unending war with his older brother. She wasn't sure what he might do or say, and she went back to the office with butterflies in her stomach.

She called the Bryant Agency in New York to check on the job, and found that she didn't have to worry. There wasn't really a job to lose. They were creating one just for her on the basis of her degree, her résumé, and the glowing description given them by her college friend, whose father was one of the agency executives. She came away feeling much better. Except that she knew for a fact that Matt was going to be stubborn about it; she knew, and she wasn't looking forward to the battle.

There was a chance that Matt would relent when he saw how capable she was. But she had to get through the next month, and she was expecting that Matt would use every weapon he had to get his own way—including the teasing, ardent manner he'd adopted with her lately. That was the most frightening of all because she had no resistance. And how could she survive living with him, watching him with women like Layne, always aware of the fact that she herself was only a passing fancy?

She'd have given anything for Matt's love, to have him care about her as she cared about him. But he was too much older, too sophisticated to give his wary heart to a little country mouse like Catherine. That hurt most of all— knowing that she hadn't a chance. It made her even more determined to get away from him.

Matt was back the next day, and Hal had been disturbingly attentive to Catherine during Matt's absence. She didn't like the look in Matt's eyes. It spelled trouble.

They were watching a recently released movie on the VCR when Matt came home that evening, wearing a khaki leisure suit with cream-colored boots and Stetson. He had the jacket slung over a shoulder, and he was smiling as he stood at the doorway and surveyed the three of them, Catherine, Betty and Hal.

"How cozy," he remarked dryly. "Just like the old days. No date, Hal?"

"Who needs a date?" Hal returned, glancing at Catherine. "The scenery's just great right here."

Catherine was watching Matt's face, and she saw it go hard when he heard the innuendo. Even Betty's enthusiastic greeting didn't bring a smile to his rigid features.

"Did you get your property?" Betty asked.

"I got it," he returned. He tossed his jacket onto a nearby chair and sat down between Hal and Catherine on the sofa, then crossed his long legs as he carelessly lit a cigarette. "How's my sale going?" he asked Catherine, sliding a casual arm behind her head.

"Very well," she said in a subdued tone, aware of Hal's probing stare beyond Matt's broad chest. She was jittery, and her voice showed it. "I, uh, just took the program to the printer's today."

"Without my approval?"

"Angel looked it over to make sure it was all right," she said. "We didn't dare wait, or we'd never get them out on time."

"Let's go over to the office," he said. "I want to check it before it goes to press."

"All right."

"How about some company?" Hal asked pointedly, rising.

Matt glared at him. "How about watching your damned movie?" he returned. "This is business."

"Oh, for sure," Hal replied mockingly.

Matt scowled, and Betty was openly staring at the three of them, her eyes as puzzled at Matt's. Only Hal and Catherine understood what was going on, and Catherine was afraid of what Matt's young brother might say next.

Hal relented all at once, laughing softly as he dropped back down on the sofa. "Okay, but don't be gone long," he joked. "I want Catherine home by midnight."

Matt's eyes darkened, narrowed, and his very stance spelled trouble. "Are you trying to say something, little brother?" he asked curtly.

"Who, me?" Hal asked innocently. "Heavens, no."

Betty had turned back to her movie with a sigh, too confused to listen anymore. Catherine felt pale, and her knees were weak, both from Hal's odd behavior and from the thought of being alone at the office with Matt. Any stolen minute with him was gold, and she'd dreaded the thought that Hal might rob her of those precious seconds.

"Then let's go," Matt told Catherine, standing aside to let her leave the room ahead of him.

She didn't look back, although she heard Hal's amused laughter as they went out of the room and into the hall. She felt chilly despite her jeans and long-sleeved white T-shirt, and she folded her arms over her breasts as they went out into the cool night air.

"Hal's in a strange mood," Matt remarked. He caught her hand as they walked, and locked her fingers into his.

She felt herself melt at the warm, rough pressure of his big hand over her small one, and involuntarily moved closer to his side. "Yes."

"Do you know why?"

She did, but she was too embarrassed to tell him what Hal had seen. "He's just being himself," she hedged.

"He'll do it once too often," came the curt reply. He looked down at her, watching her loosened hair catch the night air and blow around her face. "You look very young, Kit."

"Do I scare you off, old man?" she asked with a laugh, glancing up at him as they reached his Lincoln.

"If you come down to the office with me, it might be the other way around," he murmured seductively, jerking her by the hand so that she came right up against his warm, hard-muscled body. "I might scare you off, honey."

Wary of Hal's keen eyes, perhaps watching, she edged away from him. "Might you?"

Her sudden withdrawal seemed to puzzle him. Anger him. He dropped her hand and opened the door of the Lincoln for her. Without another word or a second glance, he walked around to his side, got in, started the car and headed down to the office.

The building was dark when they arrived. She followed him inside as he turned on the lights and strode into his office. He was ominously silent, until he suddenly whirled on his heel and pierced her with his dark, cool eyes.

"Let's have it," he said curtly. "Why the sudden ice-maiden act back there?"

She might have told him the truth if he hadn't slung his question at her, but his possessive tone, as well as his arrogance, stung. He'd been in Dallas for three days with his precious Layne, and now he was scolding Catherine for not being grateful enough for the crumbs he threw her.

"What did you expect me to do, throw myself into your arms?" she replied, glaring at him. "Isn't Layne enough, or are you just hell-bent on new conquests?"

He didn't move. Seconds later, his hands went to light a cigarette. His eyes went from it to Catherine. "I thought you were learning to trust me," he said then.

"Trust doesn't have anything to do with it," she shot back. She folded her arms across her chest. "You expect too much, Matt. I'm not part of your estate."

"Pity," he said softly, taking a draw on the cigarette. "You'd be the crowning glory, even in jeans and a T-shirt."

She flushed. He had charm all right, but

she'd be crazy to take him seriously. So she laughed. "Think so?"

He smiled, too, but it didn't reach his eyes. They seemed dull, lackluster. "Let's see what you've come up with on my cattle."

She went to the computer, fumbling a little as she fed in the program disk and then her work disk. And as luck and bad nerves would have it, what came up was the copy she didn't take to the printer—the interesting bit about the lovely young debutante heifers.

"What the hell are you trying to do to me?" Matt burst out, glaring from the white-on-black computer screen to Catherine's flushed face. "My God, Kit, I trusted you not to play at it like a schoolgirl! Do you have any idea how much work goes into cattle breeding? I'm asking one hell of a price for those cattle; who's going to take me seriously with this kind of—"

"This isn't what I took to the printer," she interrupted, standing to plead with him. "Matt, please, this was just doodling; I never meant to sabotage you." Well, she had, but that was a long time ago.

He didn't seem much calmer after her confession. His dark eyes accused, probed. "I gave you credit for being an adult," he said quietly. "But you've done everything you could lately to change my mind, haven't you, honey? I guess I've jumped the gun in more ways than just one."

She knew exactly what he meant, and she felt a sinking regret that she hadn't taken him seriously. Going out with Hal had started him doubting her, drawing away from him at the house had complicated it, and finding this foolishness in the computer had cinched it. How was she going to explain herself now? She couldn't tell him that Hal had seen them kissing the night of the wreck and had mentioned it to Catherine. God knew what he'd do to Hal if he found out. What frightened her most was a confrontation; Hal would make sure the rest of the family knew about it, and what then? It would destroy the family and make Matt look like a seducer.

"All right," he said, crushing out his cigarette. "Let's see what you showed Angel."

She fumbled around again until she got the right disk, then scrolled the records up the screen. He leaned over her shoulder to see them. His proximity bothered her, but she steeled herself not to show it. Odd how heavy his breathing sounded—but a man like Matt surely wouldn't be that disturbed by her, not when he had the sophisticated Layne on his string.

"This is what went to the printer?" he asked.

She turned her eyes to meet his, trembling inwardly at the sheer pleasure of looking at him from such a sweet distance. "Yes," she said in a husky tone.

His eyes searched hers and then went down to her mouth, studying it for a long, aching moment before he abruptly stood erect and turned away. "Okay. That's all I wanted to see. We'd better get back to the house."

She removed the disks and cut off the computer, then carefully covered it back up. She turned to him, nervous. "Matt, I'm sorry," she said hesitantly.

"It's not your fault. It's mine," he returned stonily. He glanced at her. "Maybe if I hadn't rushed you, frightened you..."

"I meant about the cattle," she began, thinking he'd misunderstood her.

"Sure. Come on, honey. I'll lock up."

But just as they started out the door, the phone rang. Matt picked it up, frowning.

"Yes!" His face froze. He glanced at Catherine with an unreadable expression as he listened, and she went taut with nerves because there was only one person who knew Matt was there. He listened, muttered something, and listened again with a face like a thunderhead. "Is that so?" he ground out finally, and the look he gave Catherine would have taken rust off a used car. "She is? Well, baby brother, you can just sit and wait!"

He slammed the phone down and glared at Catherine.

"What was that all about?" she asked, her voice weak because she had a horrible suspicion.

"That was Hal," he returned, jerking the door open. "We'd better go back to the house before he has a heart attack worrying about you. What did you tell him, Kit? That I was trying to seduce you?" he demanded with barely controlled anger.

"Matt, I wanted to tell you—"

"Forget it," he cut her off. "Hal's just

made things crystal clear for me. Let's go home.''

She went out to the car and waited for him to turn out the office lights and lock the door. She'd never felt so miserable in all her life. Hal had said something to him that had set him off, and how could she defend herself without knowing what? She knew it was only Hal's revenge for all he'd taken from Matt, but that didn't make it hurt less. He'd just killed whatever tiny chance she had with Matt, and now she wanted to kill Hal. Matt would never touch her again, never kiss the breath out of her....

She forced herself not to cry. This wouldn't do. She had to get things in perspective. Matt never wanted to marry her anyway. She'd only been a diversion, someone to play with when Layne wasn't around. She had to remember that; it would make it easier. And letting him make love to her would only have made it worse when she had to let him go. She closed her eyes, shutting out the doubts. A moment later he was beside her, starting the engine. ''You're going to have your work cut out for you," he remarked quietly as they drove back to the house.

She turned in the seat. "I don't understand."

"Don't you?" He laughed softly, glancing at her as he pulled up in front of the steps. "He needs someone strong, Kit. Someone to keep him in line. You'll find that out too late, if you aren't careful."

"Hal?" she muttered.

"Hal," he said. "I'm not blind, you know," he added when her eyes widened. "The way he fought me about you tonight, the way you froze me out...it all adds up. I should have realized when you went to Fort Worth with him that you were trying to tell me how things stood. Why in heaven's name didn't you tell me at the beginning how you felt about him?" he demanded.

"But, Matt!" she protested.

"Let it be," he said. "I hate like hell to rake over dead ashes. Almost as much as I hate being used as a substitute," he added coldly.

"But I didn't...!" she burst out.

"It doesn't matter anymore. It's over." He

finished his cigarette and put it out, and when he turned back to her, he was the stepcousin of years past. "Out, sweet cousin," he said with a grin. "I've got to call Layne. Get out of my hair."

She hadn't used him as a substitute. She loved him. But she knew that grin. It meant he was through listening. Her heart felt like two pounds of lead. He thought she loved Hal; and Hal had led her right into it. Matt didn't even seem to care—beyond a little wounded vanity. He was in too much of a hurry to hear Layne's voice. Incredible, after spending three days with her!

"All right," she replied. She studied his hard face one last time, her eyes soft and quiet and hurt. "Good night."

"Goodbye, Kit," he said in a tone like velvet.

She turned away quickly so that he wouldn't see the tears and went back into the house, alone.

Hal met her in the hall. "So there you are," he said, grinning. "Have fun?"

Without a second thought, without a whisper of remorse, she drew back her hand and slapped him across the face with the whole strength of her arm behind it.

"Damn you," she whispered shakily. "Damn you, Hal!"

He held his red cheek, his dark eyes strange as he saw the wounded fury in her flushed features, her biting eyes. "Catherine...?"

"I hope you get a dose of your own medicine," she threw at him. "I hope someday you're on the receiving end. You spend your life finding ways to hurt people, to shake them up, to get your own selfish way. You're nothing but a spoiled little boy, Hal!"

His eyes popped. Catherine had always been on his side, defending him. She didn't even look like Catherine; she was all claws and teeth and flying fur.

"But, Catherine..." he protested.

"Leave me alone!" She brushed by him and ran up the stairs to her room. Thank goodness her mother was nowhere in sight; she didn't think she could answer another question.

She cursed Hal until she ran out of breath, hating him for what he'd done. She even hated

Matt. He'd refused to listen when she'd tried
to tell him the truth.

Okay. If he wanted a war, he would have
one. But he wasn't going to find it that easy
to ignore her. She was going to show him what
he'd missed out on, and she was going to get
even with Hal if it killed her. With that
thought firmly in mind, she finally slept.

Chapter Eight

It was the longest night Catherine could ever remember. Her dreams were full of the night Matt had taken her to the movies, of the sweet anguish of being in his arms, feeling his hard mouth move so expertly on her own. It seemed like a lifetime ago, now, and he'd as good as told her that their fragile new relationship was over. It was all Hal's fault, she thought, and then realized that she'd contributed to it as well, with her childish behavior, her refusal to take Matt seriously. And perhaps he had been serious. He'd looked bleak enough last night when Hal made that horrible phone call. What if he'd felt something for her? And now she'd killed it!

The thought tormented her. If he had felt something, was it possible that she could resurrect it? Fight Layne for him and win? She got up and gave herself a pep talk as she fixed her face and dressed carefully in a white peasant dress with layers of ruffles. Perhaps it wasn't too late. But even if it was, she was going to turn over a new leaf. No more little-girl tantrums, no more stammering embarrassment. The old Catherine was going into the closet in mothballs, and the new one was going to be a force to behold. She was going to have her hair fixed, buy some new clothes. But first, she was going to stand Hal on his ear. She would see to it that he understood what he'd done to her last night.

It was late morning when she got downstairs, but oddly enough the family was still at the breakfast table. Once, Hal would have whistled blatantly when she walked in. But it was a serious, quiet Hal who looked up when she joined them.

"Morning, cousin," he said, searching her face.

"Good morning, Halbert," she returned, using his full name for the first time in memory. She smiled at him dreamily and sighed theatrically. He frowned curiously as her cool glance went to Matt. "Morning."

"Morning, sweet cousin." He grinned, not a trace of ill humor or regret in him as he leaned back in his denims to study her with the old mocking smile. "Head-hunting today, are we?"

"She did that last night," Hal murmured, touching his cheek, and he smiled tentatively. "Knocked some sense into me."

"Did it hurt?" she said with mock sorrow. "Poor darling."

Hal actually flushed, digging into his eggs with renewed vigor. He seemed to have a lot on his mind, and he kept shooting nervous glances toward Matt, who was as impassive as ever. Betty stared around her uncomprehendingly, shaking her head. She didn't understand anything they said these days. Perhaps it was the generation gap at work, cutting her off from the younger people.

"Did what hurt?" Matt asked amiably, then sipped at his second cup of coffee as he leaned back precariously in his chair, Spanish eyes dark and amused, his shirt unbuttoned at the throat and straining against the hard muscle of his chest.

"Oh, I seduced him last night, that's all," Catherine said outrageously. "Did you know he was still a virgin?"

Matt actually choked on his coffee. Hal buried his face in his hands, and Betty sat like stone, staring blankly at her daughter.

"Poor old dear," Catherine clucked as Matt coughed into his napkin. "It's your age, Matt; you just can't hold your coffee anymore."

He stopped coughing and glared at her. "What the hell's gotten into you this morning?"

"Love," she sighed, staring at Hal with a dreamy expression. "Hal, darling, when are we getting married?"

Hal's face was fascinating. It went white, then red, then purple as he gaped at her. "Married?"

"Well, I can't leave you in the lurch. I still respect you, darling," she added wickedly. "Do marry me."

"I can't," Hal burst out. "And for God's sake, stop talking about seduction!"

"Don't you like being hassled, darling?" she persisted, eyes flashing. "Doesn't it feel good to be on the receiving end?"

"Aha!" Hal burst out, sitting erect, pointing at her. "Aha, that's your game! It's revenge!"

"Darling, what have you ever done to me?" She pouted, blinking her lashes at him. "Except refuse to marry me, that is."

He threw down his napkin. "I'm leaving. I have to get to work," he said, glancing at Matt to see how the older man reacted to that bombshell. Hal grinned at his brother's puzzled expression as he stood up. "I called an old friend early this morning and begged for a job. Matt, you can scream if you like, but I'm going to work for Dan Keogh. He has a racing team, and he's letting me work my way up as a mechanic. I'm starting for minimum wage."

Matt scowled. "You? Working for minimum wage?"

Hal straightened proudly. "I'm not afraid of hard work as long as it's something I enjoy. I've always loved tinkering with cars, but I'm not cut out for real estate, despite what you promised Mother. She's dead, but I have my own life to live, and I'm going to do it my way. Cut me off without a dime if you like; I don't give a damn.'' He glanced at Catherine, who was listening intently. "You were right, Catherine,'' he added gently. "I was a selfish spoiled brat. But people can change. Just stand back and watch me. If I'm needed, I'll be at the garage. Ciao, all.''

He threw up his hand in farewell and went out the door. Matt stared after him, aghast. "I'll be damned,'' he said under his breath, fumbling for a cigarette. "A miracle!''

"Hal, working,'' Betty echoed. She lifted her napkin to her eyes. "Oh, dear, I think I'm going to cry.''

"It won't save him,'' Catherine said. "I'm still going to marry him to save his good name.''

"Darling, you didn't really...?'' Betty probed gently, all eyes.

Matt was watching, too, warily.

"I do not kiss and tell,'' Catherine said smugly. She got up, too. "I'm going to get the advertisements ready this morning, and I've got to arrange a caterer for the barbecue.'' She looked over at Matt. "Is the caterer you used last year capable?"

"Yes," he said.

"Then I'll get him again. And I need to be off for an hour at lunch," she added. "I have some shopping to do."

"Help yourself," Matt murmured, studying her curiously.

She smiled. Good. Let him guess. She was about to organize a frontal campaign, and he was the objective; but it wouldn't do to let him know it. "See you later."

"She wouldn't seduce Hal, would she?" Betty asked worriedly.

"Of course not," Matt agreed. But his eyes were narrow and thoughtful and a little worried as he watched her flounce out of the room.

Catherine was humming softly at the computer when Matt came in. Hold on to your heart, girl, she told herself, and steeled herself not to jump or blush when he stood over her.

"Almost through," she told him with a sunny smile. "Angel said the printer would like you to look over the layout before he prints your programs."

"I'll go now," he said. He stared down at her, his hands in the pockets of his tight jeans, his dark eyes shaded by his straw hat, his face impassive. "You haven't slept with Hal have you?"

She looked up at him sensuously. "Darling, haven't I?" she returned huskily, smiling slowly at the darkness growing in his eyes.

He started to say something, clammed up and slammed out of the office. Catherine only smiled.

She went into town at lunch hour and wandered into a hairdressing salon that specialized in walk-in customers. Twenty minutes later she walked back out into the sun with a wavy short haircut that added years of sophistication to her face, emphasizing her big green eyes and pretty, pouting mouth. She laughed, feeling new and excited. She went to a large department store next and smothered her very traditional instincts. She bought gauzy blouses, low-cut in front, and flaring skirts. She bought slinky dresses and an off-the-shoulder evening gown in a wild jungle-green print. She bought open-toed high heels and sandals and some trendy earrings. And before she went back to work, she donned one of the new outfits—a swirling blue gauze skirt and a deeply cut, puffy-sleeved white blouse. With a touch of red lipstick and some eye makeup she'd never used and big, flashy blue earrings, she looked like something out of *Vogue*. She laughed at her reflection, wondering at the change. And then she went back to work.

The expression on Matt's dark face when he came back from lunch was comical. He stopped in the doorway and stared, just as Angel and the other girls had, but he took longer to recover.

"Well?" she asked huskily, smiling provocatively at him. "Do you like it?"

"My God, you can't come to work dressed like that," he said curtly. He closed the door and jerked out a cigarette.

"You smoke too much, darling," she murmured. She got up and went close to him, winding veils of seductive perfume around him as she gently took the cigarette from his fingers. She was awed by the way he reacted.

"Kit," he said under his breath. His eyes went to the bodice of the blouse, to the deep V that left her smooth breasts revealed.

"What's wrong, cowboy?" she asked, staring up into his darkened eyes. "Do I bother you?"

"Of course you bother me!" he growled. His hands caught her waist and squeezed, pulling her against him. "Why?"

"Why what?" she asked, parting her lips and watching his eyes rivet to them.

"The haircut. The new clothes," he said. "Is this for Hal's benefit? If it is, you'd better lock your door at night, or you may catch the wrong fly, little spider."

"I couldn't catch you," she whispered. "You've got Layne, haven't you?"

He couldn't seem to get his breath. His hands moved up her sides to her rib cage, feeling the softness of her skin through the flimsy blouse. "Kit..."

She arched her throat, her eyes half closed, lazy. She linked her hands around his neck and swayed back against his arms. "Like it?"

"Fire," he whispered roughly. "Fire, Kit, and you're more flammable than you might think."

"Then burn me," she whispered back, going up on tiptoe to tempt his hard mouth. Her heart throbbed in her chest; her knees felt weak as she experienced the hardness of his lean body against hers. "Burn me, Matthew."

"Oh, God...!" he ground out. His mouth opened as it took hers in a kiss that should have been violent and wasn't. It was a tender taking, a shivery seduction of lips against tender lips, and his mouth trembled with the hunger it aroused in him.

She caught her breath, feeling sensations she'd never experienced before, not even with Matt. Her fingers tangled in the fabric of his denim shirt, holding on as her body began to shudder where it felt the hot imprint of his muscles.

"Open your mouth, baby," he whispered shakily as he moved her closer.

She did, feeling his tongue enter her, her eyes closing as the magic worked and the fires burned. Vaguely, she felt his arms contracting hungrily, grinding her against his aroused body, but her mind was in flames. She reached up and clung to him, her teeth nibbling at his hard mouth, her tongue fencing with his in an intimacy that defied restraint. She moaned, a sound like a whispered scream, and he lifted his head to look at her.

"I've never heard that before," he whispered as he brushed her mouth again with his. "Haven't I aroused you before this?"

"Wh-what?" She tried to think, but it was all she could do to speak.

"That sweet little sound you made," he murmured against her searching lips. "Women make it in passion, when they make love with men and the feeling breaks through. And sometimes, when men do this to them...." His hand moved, his fingers seeking out the hard tip of her breast and teasing around it in a tender searching that brought the sound again.

She looked up at him in a fever. There were too many clothes between them. She wanted to lie down with him and touch his skin. Feel him touching hers. Kissing it. His mouth on her bareness...

"Oh, no," he whispered, laughing softly as he read the thought in her eyes. "No, not here. I don't want an audience."

"Audience?" she echoed, arching to the subtle magic his fingers were working on her body. "Matt..." she moaned, straining to hold that exquisite touch.

He brushed soft kisses against her nose. "Is this what you're trying so hard to make me do?" he asked tenderly, and eased her head gently against his shoulder. His hand lifted, and he turned his eyes downward and watched as his fingers slid inside her blouse, into the deep V neck, and traced patterns on her bare skin.

"Low...lower," she whispered shamelessly, on fire for him.

His breath came as quickly as her own. He held her eyes. "Here?" he breathed, as she felt his fingers searching for the hardness.

She trembled and gasped as he found it, and he watched her face go hot with the tiny consummation. His hand flattened against her breast, taking the hard nipple into his moist palm, molding her while she clung to him and bit her lip to keep from crying out.

"Kit," he whispered achingly. He bent and put his mouth slowly on hers and, teasing her lips apart, tasted the heady mint of her breath. His hand squeezed and she made a sound that stiffened his taut body, that sent his free hand low on her spine to grind her hips into his.

Her mouth opened under the hunger of his, and she reached up and clung to him glorying in the blatant message his body was relaying to her as he bruised her body into his in a slow, hungry rhythm.

She felt him shudder and pressed closer, trembling the length of her body, aching in places she'd never realized were so sensitive, moaning as she longed for something to end the anguished pleasure that was so new and unbearable....

"No!" He caught her arms and thrust her roughly away from him. "No!" he said hoarsely. He shuddered again, his face unrecognizable in passion, dark and black-eyed and rigid with unsatisfied hunger.

"Matt?" she whispered, staring up at him with her red, swollen mouth parted, tempting, her arms half lifted, her eyes yielding already.

With a harsh groan, he turned away, pressing his hands against the desk, leaning on them for support, his body in a stiff arch. "Get me a whiskey, Kit," he said in a voice thick with pain.

She stood there for a second, trying to get her mind back. She could hardly wobble over to the bar to do as he asked, her legs were trembling so. She poured a measure of whiskey into a shot glass, spilling some of it, and impulsively took a sip. It was hot in her throat, but she got it down and felt it steadying her.

She carried the glass to Matt, and when he didn't take it, she set it on the desk between his outstretched hands.

He took deep, ragged breaths, and Kit began to realize what was wrong with him. Her face went beet red as she remembered what they'd been doing, remembered the effect she could have on his body.

"I'm sorry," she whispered.

He straightened and picked up the whiskey, draining it in a single swallow. His face was pale and strained, and he looked violent. It was a full minute before he turned toward her.

"I won't die," he said when he saw the concern in her eyes. "You threw me off balance, that's all. You've seen it happen before," he reminded her.

"Yes. But not like that." Her gaze lowered to his shuddering chest.

"Not even with Hal?" he asked with a harsh laugh. "Poor boy."

"I don't feel like this with Hal," she blurted out, compounding the problem.

"Love without lust? How puritan," he scoffed. He jerked out a cigarette and lit it. "From now on, keep your attempts at seduction for your victim, Kit, and keep away from me, will you? As you've just seen, I'm pretty vulnerable."

She knew he hated admitting that. Her eyes searched his. "I'm just as vulnerable," she reminded him. "It wasn't just you."

"I realize that. But I'm no more inclined toward marriage than Hal seems to be," he added coldly. "On the other hand, I'm old-fashioned enough that I'd marry you if we made love, so save us both a lot of heartache and practice your wiles elsewhere."

"I thought you believed I'd already succeeded," she probed.

He searched her blushing face. "Kit, I'm not a virgin. I can recognize experience. You don't have it. Not in the way I mean."

"Ah, one of those experts who can recognize innocence with a look?" she teased.

"People who've had sex can control their hungers a little easier," he said tautly.

Her eyebrows arched. "Are you a virgin, too? You didn't seem that much in control to me."

He took a sharp breath. "Catherine...!"

She smiled at him, more confident now than she'd ever been before. Layne evidently wasn't giving him all he needed, or why would he have been so hungry? That gave her hope.

"Next time, I'll be more careful with you, darling," she whispered. "But right now, I have to get back to work."

He didn't seem to have a reply. He puffed on his cigarette while she went back to her computer and picked up where she'd left off.

She glanced up at him with an impish grin. "Feeling better?" she murmured.

"Not a lot, no," he returned. His chest rose and fell heavily as he smoked, and his eyes went over her. "You've grown up with a vengeance, haven't you?"

"It happens to the best of us." She glanced at him meaningfully. "Convinced now that I can handle myself in New York? If you aren't,

I'll prove it to you by the time we have the barbecue.''

His face clouded over. "How? By seducing Hal and me?''

"Hal won't let me seduce him," she sighed, darting a look up at him. "But you might."

His eyes flashed at her, and despite himself, he smiled. "Think so?''

"Look out," she warned softly. "I'm dangerous.''

He held up the empty whiskey glass. "So I've seen. But there's something you'd better remember.''

"Oh? What?''

He put the glass down and leaned over her, enveloping her in his spicy cologne. "I'm dangerous, too." He broke her mouth open under his, but before she could drown in the sweet pleasure, he lifted his head and, with a wink, went out the door.

Chapter Nine

Betty was delighted with her daughter's new look. She raved about it when Catherine came home that night.

"You look so different, darling," she exclaimed, smiling at her only child.

"I grew up," Catherine replied, bending to kiss her mother's soft cheek.

"Not quite," Matt murmured as he strode past them toward the study.

"Matthew!" Catherine grumbled, glaring after him.

"And I remember the last time you called me that," he returned, grinning at her. "Do you?"

She did, and her mother's eyebrows arched at the red blush in Catherine's cheeks.

"I do wish I understood what's going on around here," Betty sighed.

The front door opened and Hal came in, grimy and grease stained and smiling from ear to ear. "I'm home!" he called.

"Wonderful!" Catherine greeted him. "Shall I call the minister now, or do you want to wash up first?"

Hal stared at her. "Now, Catherine..."

"I owe it to you to make an honest man of you," she told him. "Now, let's see, it can't be until after the barbecue, or Matt would never forgive us."

"Damned straight," Matt shouted from the den.

"But it will have to be before I leave for New York," she continued, frowning thoughtfully.

"You can forget New York," Matt called. "There are enough professional troublemakers up there without Texas imports."

"I will not forget it," she returned. "The whole point of my going to work for you was to prove that I can take care of myself."

"You haven't yet," he said.

She glared toward his study. "Will you please stop interrupting. I'm trying to set a wedding date in here."

"Sure, honey. I'll be your flower girl," Matt promised.

Betty burst out laughing and winked at Hal, who still wasn't sure whether to laugh or cry.

"Will you wear a pink taffeta dress, Matt, dear?" Catherine baited.

"If you marry Hal, I will."

Hal tried unsuccessfully to smother a grin. "Oh, Catherine," he chuckled. "It would almost be worth my freedom to see Matt in pink taffeta."

"Hal, I'm delighted to hear you say that," Catherine said with a smile. "Now, when do we set the date?"

"On your fifty-sixth birthday. I promise." He held his hand over his heart.

"Well," she said, pretending to consider his offer.

Hal came closer, and brushed a brotherly kiss against her forehead. "Forgive me," he said gently. "I've learned my lesson. And for what it's worth, I'm sorry."

She searched his dark eyes consideringly. "It's a little late for that."

"Do you think so?" he murmured, glancing deliberately toward the den. "I'm not so sure."

"Anyway," she said changing the subject and turning away, "I don't have time to marry you now, Hal. I'm going to be too busy. Matt, I called the caterer, and I've got the invitations ready to address. Angel and I will start on them tomorrow."

"Okay, honey," he replied.

"I'd better get cleaned up for dinner."

"Annie's waiting to bring in the first course," Betty told everyone, "so let's hurry."

The doorbell rang as Hal went upstairs, and Betty opened the door to let Jerry and Barrie come in.

"Hello, everyone, I hope we're not intruding," Barrie said, flashing a blue-eyed smile at them, "but we have news."

"Big news," Jerry agreed with a grin at his redheaded wife.

"This sounds serious," Catherine said, staring at them. She glanced at Barrie. "Are you expecting?"

"Yes!" Barrie answered, clasping her hands in front of her. "Oh, I'm so excited, I don't know what to do. I've waited so long, and Jerry finally agreed—Catherine, how different you look! I love your hair!"

"Thank you," came the demure reply. "But tell us about you. When is it due?"

"Tomorrow," Barrie said dreamily.

Catherine looked at her flat stomach with wide, unblinking eyes. "Tomorrow?"

"Tomorrow?" Betty echoed with the same astonished look.

Barrie grimaced when she saw where all the eyes were staring. "Not that!" she burst out. "My goodness, not a baby! My herd of cattle!"

Catherine turned away, shaking her head. "I don't believe this. She comes in talking about exciting big news; we think it's a baby, and it's cattle!"

"She wouldn't get that excited over a baby," Jerry sighed, putting an arm around his petite wife. "But Lord, she does love cattle, and I made this great deal on a small herd of purebred Santa Gertrudis.''

"Santa Gertrudis!" Matt came storming out of his office. "Like hell you're running Santa Gertrudis next to my purebred Herefords!"

"Now, Matt," Barrie said quickly, "I've got good fences."

"I've seen bulls that can get through a six-foot fence," he returned. "I don't want my purebred cows mixing with other strains; you'll ruin my breeding program!"

"I told you," Jerry groaned.

Barrie smiled at Matt, blinking her big blue eyes. "Now, Matt, I won't put them anywhere near your stock. Why, I've rented some land six miles away, just to keep my cattle on."

"You have?" Jerry asked.

"I have," Barrie said smugly. She grinned at her husband. "I told you I'd have all my bases covered. Jack Halston is renting me his bottoms.''

"Bottoms," Matt sighed. "Honey, the first flash flood will take out your whole investment.''

"There's some high ground nearby," she

said. "I checked. It will work out just fine. I'm so excited! My own herd!"

"Some herd." Jerry chuckled. "Six cows and a bull."

"It's a start," she returned. She lifted her head and sniffed. "Steak! Country-fried steak and mashed potatoes. Oh, my, are we in time for supper? Is there enough? I'm just starved!"

"As usual," Annie observed, bustling to the table with platters of food. "Yes, there's enough. Come on before I chuck it out the back door."

Conversation for the rest of the evening centered on Barrie's cattle. Even Hal seemed to be excited for her. He took time to share his own news about his first day on the job.

"I'm doing fine, Keogh says. He's going to let me run a lap on Saturday on the track. I can hardly wait," he said fervently.

"Just make sure there aren't any embankments nearby," Matt murmured with a wink, leaning back with a brandy in his lean hand.

"Oh, I'll watch myself from now on, for sure," Hal promised. He glanced at Catherine with a smile.

"Stop leering at me, if you please," Catherine said huffily. "Just because I seduced you once is no reason to expect it from now on."

"Will you stop telling people you've seduced me!" Hal burst out as Barrie and Jerry gaped at him. "It isn't true!"

"You told Matt I did," she said, taking a shot in the dark as she remembered the telephone call at the office the night Matt came back from Dallas.

"I lied," Hal grumbled, glancing at Matt. "It was a practical joke, and I'll be the first to admit it backfired. I was out for revenge, but I'm the one who got kicked. I surrender, Catherine."

"It's no use," she said wistfully. "I'm just not in the mood tonight. I have a headache."

"Will you quit that!" Hal moaned.

Matt was watching with curious dark eyes. He studied Catherine quietly, intently as he sipped his brandy.

She glanced at him, then turned away. Well, he needn't think that anything had really changed just because she'd made Hal admit the truth. She knew Matt wanted her, but there were still Layne and Matt's obsession with freedom. She'd only wanted to clear the slate, she told herself. But deep inside, she wondered what Matt would do now—if he'd do anything.

Matt didn't say another word until Barrie and Jerry had gone home and Hal had gone up to bed. Betty was doing embroidery, and Matt got up and announced that he was going to sit on the porch swing, and asked wouldn't Catherine like some air?

She would, she agreed, but as she said good-night to Barrie and followed him outside, it was with apprehension.

As it turned out, she didn't have any reason to worry. Because he seemed to have more important things on his mind than romance under the stars.

"Sit down, honey. I won't bite," he said wickedly when she hesitated.

She plopped down beside him and felt his long legs rock the swing into a rhythmic, creaking motion. Nearby, crickets sang, and from far in the distance came the sound of cars going along the highway. With a sigh, Catherine leaned her head back against Matt's muscular arm and closed her eyes.

"How did you know what Hal said to me that night?" he asked after a while.

"I didn't. I took a lucky shot."

"He has a vindictive streak a mile wide," he remarked.

"Yes, but it's just as well," she said lazily, opening her eyes to smile up at his shadowed face. "You'd only have seduced me and hated yourself."

"Think so?" he murmured, glancing down at her.

"I know so. Sex isn't a good basis for a relationship. I may be green, but I know that much."

His fingers toyed with her hair. "I'm not sure I like it this short," he remarked.

"They'll like it in New York," she assured him.

"You're still determined that you want to go?"

"Yes," she lied, suddenly unsure about her answer.

He lit a cigarette and took a long draw from it. "Don't you like working with Angel and the other girls?"

"I like it very well. But I don't plan to

spend the rest of my life here, Matt. I'm not like Barrie. Cattle don't mean the world to me.''

"It's all been a game with you, has it?"

"What has?"

He stared out into the darkness. "Playing me off against Hal."

"I wasn't," she protested. She shifted her head against his arm to stare up at him. "You're the one who likes to play around, big cousin, you with your harem. You draw women like flies."

"A certain type of woman," he corrected. He drew on the cigarette, and she could see his hard, even profile in the red glow. "And for all you know, they could have been window dressing, young Catherine. I might have lived like a monk for the past two years."

"Elephants might fly," she replied. "You aren't the monkish type."

His eyes sought hers in the dim light coming from the windows. "Maybe I only want one woman."

"Yes," she said quietly. "The oh-so-sophisticated Layne, of course."

He paused for an instant before he spoke.

"You've never been curious about my women before, Kit."

That was true enough. "I've never been an adult before," she replied gradually.

"You aren't yet, either," he murmured deeply. "What you know about men and sex could be written on the head of a straight pin."

"Getting experience wasn't easy with you and Mother bulldogging me," she replied.

"The only experience you've got, I've given you," he said under his breath. He looked down at her, his dark, warm eyes searching over her flushed face. "And it's only beginning."

"No, it isn't," she shot at him. "I won't be a plaything!" She jerked away from him and got to her feet.

"So nervous," he said gently. "So frightened. And if you'd open your eyes, Kit, you'd realize there's nothing to be afraid of."

"That's what you think!"

"It won't hurt that much," he said in a tone that sent chills down her spine. "Maybe not at all. I can be gentle."

She went red and, choking on the attempt

to fire back at him, she whirled and stormed back inside to the sound of his predatory laughter.

Whether it was a blessing in disguise or a curse, Catherine was much too busy in the following days to fence with Matt. Organizing the public relations end of the sale was the hardest work she'd ever done. There was one detail after another to see to, and getting out the invitations took the better part of two days. Ads had to be worked out for newspapers and trade magazines; there were the logistics of seating the crowds, name tags to buy, all the thousand and one tiny headaches that accompanied fitting out the ranch for the large number of guests.

"We'll never get through addressing envelopes," Angel wailed at the end of a particularly long day, "and I thought we were all finished!"

"I know," Catherine said wearily. "Well, maybe now we are."

The office door opened and Hal came in, looking flashy in slacks and a patterned blue shirt. "Hi," he said. "Thought I'd look in on my way to Fort Worth for the races. Care to go with me, Kit?''

She was tempted, but there were still bits and pieces to coordinate. ''Thanks anyway,'' she said with a smile, ''but I'm too far behind.''

''How dreadful,'' Hal sighed. ''Here I am, in my first trial, and there's nobody to cheer me on.'' He stuck his hands in his pockets and shot a curious glance at Angel, who seemed unusually intent on her typewriter. ''Say, Angel, do you like auto racing?''

Angel's eyes came up, big and black and nervous. ''Why, yes,'' she answered hesitantly. ''My uncle used to race.''

Hal grinned. ''Want to come to Fort Worth with me?'' he asked softly. ''We could go out to dinner afterward.''

''Well…''

''Go!'' Catherine coaxed. ''Matt won't say anything. After all, it's Saturday. We've both been working overtime, you know.''

Angel smiled shyly at Hal. ''In that case, I'd love to go with you. Should I change?''

Hal studied the pretty floral dress she was

wearing and slowly shook his head. "No way, honey. You look terrific."

Angel actually blushed, not at all the cool, competent young woman Catherine had come to know. She had to hide a smile as they left, already deep in conversation.

Matt sauntered in minutes later, a puzzled frown crossing his face when he saw Catherine working alone.

"Did your help desert you?" he asked.

"She went off with Hal to cheer him to victory," Catherine answered. "I told her I was sure you wouldn't mind."

"I do mind," he said shortly. "You know Hal. I don't want to lose the best secretary I've ever had. He's a lady-killer."

"Just look who's talking," Catherine chided, glaring up at him.

His dark eyes traveled slowly over the low-cut white blouse and gray slacks she was wearing, the perky gray dotted scarf at her throat. "I don't kill them, honey. I seduce them," he said in a wicked undertone.

"Hal won't seduce Angel," she promised him. "She knows karate."

"Fat lot of good it will do her," he murmured, "if Hal turns on the heat."

"Men are a conceited lot," she remarked as she finished the last envelope and put it beside the printer. "Boy, am I tired!"

"Suppose you come out to supper with me."

She stared up at him uncertainly. "I don't know."

"I'll buy you fried oysters, Kit," he coaxed.

"For fried oysters, I'll come," she said, getting up and covering the printer. "But where are we going to find them around here?"

Two hours later, dining in an exclusive restaurant in Galveston, she didn't have to repeat the question. Matt had hustled her off to the airport and they'd flown there in his private plane.

"I'm not really dressed for this," she murmured, glancing around at all the elegantly dressed women.

"You look fine to me, honey," he replied. He leaned back with a glass of Chablis in his lean hand, studying her across the white tablecloth. He was wearing slacks, a white turtleneck shirt and a blue blazer. He'd added the blazer in the plane; apparently he kept it there for just such emergencies.

"The barbecue's set," she told him.

"No business talk," he said. "Tonight, we're just a man and a women."

"How exciting," she said with a smile. "What are we going to do?"

"That's a leading question." He sipped his wine. "What would you like to do, Catherine?"

"I think I'd like to be one of your women, just for a night," she said, but it was pure bravado; she'd had two glasses of wine and she shouldn't have.

"How do you think my evenings end, when I take out that kind of woman?"

She finished her second glass of wine. "I have a pretty good idea, and that's not what I meant."

He toyed with his glass, pursing his chiseled lips as he stared across at her. "We could start with some slow dancing," he suggested.

"That sounds safe enough."

It did, until Matt took her in his arms on the small dance floor while a live band played lazy blues tunes. He held her with both arms, while she linked hers around his neck. Although she'd gone to plenty of college parties, Catherine had never danced so close to a man she wanted. And she learned quickly that it was an intoxicating experience. It made her knees weak, made her body throb where it brushed so intimately against his. She looked up with all her uncertainties plain in her wide green eyes.

"Don't be nervous," he said gently, leaning down to brush his mouth over her forehead. "Think of it as making love to music."

"That's what it feels like, Matt," she whispered, inhaling the clean, spicy scent of his skin, feeling the warm strength of his body.

"Yes, I know." He made a sharp turn, and she felt his thigh against her own and trembled. "Do you like that?" he asked at her ear and did it again.

"Oh, Matt," she whispered shakily, clinging closer. She couldn't seem to help herself; she wanted to be as near him as she could get. Her body ached with needs she was only now discovering.

His teeth found her ear and nibbled it

gently. "I've got an apartment here," he whispered.

"H-have you?"

"We could go there."

Give me strength, she prayed. Her eyes shut tight. "No."

"I wouldn't hurt you," he breathed.

Her legs trembled against his. "Don't ask me."

"I want you."

"I know. But I can't."

He laughed softly. "Can't you? I thought you were a modern girl, Kit. Or didn't you know that this is how it's going to be in New York? People hand out sex like a party favor in the circles you'll be traveling in."

She drew a little away from him and searched his mocking eyes. "Is that why you asked me? Is this an object lesson?"

"I think you need one, little innocent," he said quietly.

"Then suppose you take me to your apartment, Matt, and teach me how to survive in the big city?" she challenged.

He held her at arm's length a moment, and his dark eyes cut into hers, then ran down her slender body. Suddenly he pressed her close again, his hands clutching at her back. "I could teach you plenty," he breathed. "But nothing would be the same afterward. Not between us, or with the family. And I could get you pregnant."

She felt her cheeks go hot. "I thought men knew how to prevent it."

"There are only two ways a man has," he said gently, searching her eyes. "One is reliable but uncomfortable, and the other is uncertain at best. The best prevention I know of is strolling birth control," he added with a wicked grin. "But you won't go to movies with me these days."

She hid her face against his broad chest, nuzzling him, feeling his strength as they circled the dance floor. She was throbbing with forbidden hungers, wanting nothing more than to lie with him in a big, cool bed and learn all the secrets, solve the mystery.

His lean hand smoothed over her back, warm and strong through the silky blouse, his fingers wandering from her neck to her waist. "Kit, are you wearing a bra?" he asked in a sultry whisper.

She felt her breasts going taut. "No," she replied.

He tensed as they moved slowly to the music. "That's too bad. Because when we get back to the plane, I'm going to take off this blouse and look at you."

Her eyes came up, wide and shocked, and he held them ruthlessly, his body hard against hers, his hands seductively caressing her back.

"You don't want to stay here any more than I do," he said huskily. "Let's go."

She didn't remember leaving the restaurant or the slow cab ride back to the plane. She was burning as if with a fever and was totally beyond rational thought.

Matt paid the cabdriver and let her go into the plane while he walked around in the craft, checking it out. But when he finally got in and closed up the plane, it wasn't to taxi out onto the runway.

He bent and lifted Catherine in his strong arms and sank into one of the wide, comfortable seats with her on his lap.

"Now," he whispered, "we can have dessert."

And as he finished speaking, his mouth

crushed gently against hers, opening it to a slow, probing kiss. His free hand moved to her silky blouse, easing each button delicately from its buttonhole while she watched his face in a silence thick with desire.

He slowly peeled the blouse away from her taut, swollen breasts, and she lay quietly in his arms and let him look at her.

"My God, you're lovely," he whispered with something like reverence in his tone. "I'm almost afraid to touch you, Catherine."

His fingers went down to her collarbone and traced patterns there. Her lips parted on a held breath as his fingers moved down slowly, lazily.

"You feel like silk, baby," he breathed, letting his eyes follow the seductive movement of his fingers. "Except for these...so hard to the touch."

He touched her nipples and watched her arch at the exquisite pleasure.

"Kit, I thought I had so much patience," he whispered ruefully. He moved, lifting her up to his mouth. "But I'm hungry, too."

He took one small, perfect breast right into his mouth, creating a warm, moist suction that made her cry out in a voice she didn't recognize.

It was a maelstrom of feeling, of shocked pleasure, of anguished desire. She clung and cried while he devoured her from the waist up, letting her feel his tongue, his teeth. And it was the most beautiful experience of her entire life.

"Matt," she whispered, her trembling hands in his dark hair, holding his mouth against her. "Oh, Matt, I never dreamed, never thought...!"

"I love the taste of you, baby," he whispered against her body. "I love the smell of you, the sweet softness of you. Kit, I want you so!"

His mouth slid up her chin to cover her mouth, and he drew her against him, feeling her searching hands frantically lifting the bottom of his shirt so that her skin could merge with his hair-roughened chest. He shuddered as he felt her sinking against him, the warm, hard-tipped softness crushing so exquisitely into his hard muscles.

"I could die and I wouldn't mind now,"

she whispered huskily, clinging to him. "Oh, Matt, it feels so sweet...!"

"I know." His arms tightened, and he ground her against him, rocking her gently, his mouth over hers, shuddering with the tenderness of a kiss that shook them both with its soft intensity.

"Silky little virgin," he whispered unsteadily, "you don't know how dangerous this is."

"You said you wanted me," she reminded him, glorying in the pleasure they were creating.

"I did. I do. And you want me. But we can't make love for the first time in a parked airplane, Kit."

"Why not?" she asked mindlessly, looking up at him with pleading eyes.

He caught his breath, letting her slide down into the crook of his arm so that he could feast his eyes on her sweet nudity. "God, you're so exquisite, Kit!" he whispered, touching her delicately so that she shuddered with pleasure.

"I want you," she whispered.

"Yes. But not like this," he whispered back. He bent and kissed her eyelids closed, and then he buttoned her blouse, slowly, reluctantly. "When it happens, I want it in bed, in private, so that we have all night to enjoy each other."

"When?" she whispered.

"Soon." He bent and brushed his mouth over hers. "But right now, we have to get home. And I can't fly with you in my arms, honey. I'd crash the plane."

He eased her into a sitting position. "Come sit with me in the cockpit."

She followed him, and let him strap her into the seat before he got into his own and put on the headphones. He flashed her a smile, and minutes later they were airborne.

It didn't take long to get back to the ranch. The lights were all out except for one in the living room and one on the front porch, and when they got inside, it was to find Hal sitting up alone.

"Betty's gone to play bridge with friends," he told them. "And I've just taken Angel home," he added with a strangely shy grin. "You two have fun?"

"We had oysters in Galveston," Catherine volunteered.

"How interesting," he commented with a grin.

"Stop that or I'll make you marry me," Catherine threatened.

"Okay, I'll behave," he sighed.

"Good night. Thanks for the dinner," Catherine told Matt, a little disappointed that they didn't have the house to themselves—and her eyes told him so.

"Good night, little cousin," he said with a smile full of tenderness and memories.

She climbed the stairs reluctantly and got ready for bed. Minutes later, there was a light tap on the door. She opened it to find Hal outside.

"Matt says, will you trade rooms with him for tonight," Hal said softly. "He says he wants to keep an eye on those new cattle of Barrie's, and he can look out your window and see them."

What an odd request, she thought, but she was so full of wine that it never registered just how strange the request was. "Okay," she said, yawning, and pulled on her robe.

She climbed into Matt's huge bed in the dark and was almost instantly asleep. So it came as a shock the next morning when she opened her eyes and found Matt sound asleep beside her—apparently without a stitch of clothing on, if his broad chest and flat stomach showing above the precarious sheet were any indication.

She sat up in bed, feeling woolly-headed from the night before, and stared down at him with her gown half off one shoulder. And just as she touched his chest to wake him, the door opened and there stood Betty, a cup of tea in her hand and disbelief on her face.

Chapter Ten

Betty stood for long moments like a statue in the doorway. Then she leaned forward, blinking, the cup of coffee hanging precariously in her fingers. She frowned, shook her head and went back out, leaving the door open.

"Matt, wake up!" Catherine squealed in a whisper. She shook him, feeling warm, hard muscle and rough skin and wanting to touch so much more than his broad shoulders.

His eyes opened slowly, looking up into hers. He smiled lazily. "Well, hello, angel. Did I die in my sleep?"

"What are you doing in here?" she burst out.

"It's my bedroom. I think." He sat up, disrupting the cover, and Catherine had a brief, shocking glimpse of what was under the sheet. "Yep, this is my bedroom, all right. What are you doing in it?" he added blankly, staring at her.

"Will you cover yourself up!" she groaned, averting her eyes and her feverish cheeks while he chuckled and dashed the sheet back over his hips.

Outside in the hall there were voices. Matt's eyebrows arched as Betty came back with Hal in tow.

"You see?" Betty murmured, indicating the two still figures in bed. "I told you so."

Hal peered at them, too. "I'm not sure. Maybe it's an illusion. I drank last night. So did Matt."

"That is not an illusion," Betty grumbled. She glanced at Matt and Catherine. "I'll get the others."

"My God, are you selling tickets?" Matt growled at their retreating backs. He turned to Catherine. "What are you doing in my bed?"

"Hal said you wanted to swap rooms with me, so you could watch over Barrie's cattle," she said, then cleared her throat when, cold sober, she realized how stupid that sounded. "I've been had."

"It looks that way, and guess who they'll think has had you?" Matt returned sharply, his dark eyes going over her breasts, which were visible through the nearly-transparent blue gown she was wearing. "My, my, Kit, do you always sleep like that?" he added in a seductive tone.

"Stop gaping at me," she muttered.

"You like it, you little coward," he returned. He reached up and brushed his fingers lightly over her breasts, watching her breath catch, her face mirror the shock of pleasure. He reached up and slid his fingers into her short hair. "Come down here."

"Matt—" she started to protest just as voices came closer again.

"Oh, hell," he growled, throwing himself flat on his back. "I feel like a museum exhibit."

Catherine's eyes went over his long, hardmuscled body with smiling awe. "You look better than any painting I've ever seen," she confessed, "even without a fig leaf."

"Kit!"

She averted her face, stunned at her own remark. "Sorry."

The doorway suddenly filled with faces. "See?" Betty was telling the others. Barrie and Jerry stared. So did Hal. They all murmured and pointed and frowned.

Matt groaned and pulled the cover over his face.

"Stop that!" Catherine grumbled at him. "It's all your fault, anyway. Why did you have to come sleep in here?"

"It's my damned bed!" Matt said gruffly from under the sheet.

"That's no excuse," Catherine returned curtly. She glanced at the onlookers. "Hal did it!" she accused, pointing at him. "He told me Matt wanted to trade rooms."

"Me?" Hal burst out, gaping. "I never!"

Catherine's jaw fell. "You did, you liar! You came and knocked on my door and told me Matt wanted me to sleep in his room!"

"I," Hal replied, "am an innocent bystander, being falsely accused."

"I never thought I'd live to see Matt and Catherine in bed together," Jerry remarked.

"Same here," Barrie replied.

"Shocking." Angel clicked her tongue, grinning wickedly. Angel!

"How many people did you bring in with you, Mother!" Catherine asked in what she hoped was a calm tone, although her voice sounded two octaves higher than normal.

"Well, just family, darling," Betty defended herself. "And Angel, and Mr. Bealy, here—he's come to see Matt about a bull."

"Pleased to meet you, ma'am." Mr. Bealy, a middle-aged man, grinned, doffing his hat.

"And Miss Harley, of course," Betty added, introducing a lovely little old lady who occasionally visited Betty.

"Nice to see you again, Catherine," Miss Harley said with a smile.

Catherine glanced from them to the mumbling lump beside her in bed. With a weary sigh, she lay down and pulled the cover over her head, too.

"Nobody will believe the truth in this house," she wailed.

"What did I tell you?" Matt agreed, grinning at her under the sheet.

"I'll have breakfast when you two are hungry, dear,'' Betty called gaily as the crowd went out. "No hurry." The door closed.

"My reputation is ruined," Catherine wailed. "Hal lied!"

Matt threw off the sheet. "Well, Kit, so much for New York."

"No! Now is the best time for me to go there!" she protested.

He moved, arching over her, resting his weight on his arms. "No it isn't honey," he murmured with a soft laugh. "Now is the best time for us to announce our engagement—before this sordid story gets spread all over southern Oklahoma and northern Texas."

"Engagement?" Her heart leaped wildly. "You're not serious."

"Yes, I am." He bent and brushed her mouth lazily with his. "You want me, Kit. And I want you. The rest will come naturally. We'll get married and make babies and raise cattle."

Her pulse was going wild. "But—"

His mouth opened on hers. His chest came down over her breasts, crushing them gently, his hands smoothing down her sides to her hips. Abruptly he turned on his side, jerking her body completely against his.

She gasped, her eyes wide open in shock at the contact with his hard body, only the flimsy film of her gown between them.

"Kit," he breathed, his eyes dark as she'd never before seen them, a tremor in the arms that urged her even closer. "God, you're so soft. Velvet and silk and magic in my arms."

"Matt, you don't...have any clothes on," she faltered.

He searched her eyes. "We could take your gown off," he whispered. "We could feel each other like this."

Her lips trembled. "No."

"You want to," he whispered, leaning nearer to brush her eyes closed with his mouth. "Don't you?"

His hands were on her body, on the long line of her back, her hips, her upper thighs. She trembled, and he smiled against her forehead, nudging her body against his in a slow, torturous rhythm, letting her feel what she already knew, that he wanted her obsessively.

"Oh...Matt..." Her voice broke as the sensations grew unmanageable. Her hands went to his chest, trembling as they pressed into thick hair and hard muscle.

"Don't stop there," he whispered at her mouth. "Touch me. Learn my body, as I'm learning yours."

She started to protest, but he moved, guiding her hands, watching her face as she learned the most private things about him. Her eyes grew enormous, but she didn't fight him.

He smiled at her shocked fascination, laughing even as he trembled with pleasure. "Marry me, Kit," he breathed, "and I'll let you have me."

"Tease," she returned, barely able to manage laughter herself.

"Don't you want me, honey?" He brushed his mouth lazily over hers, feeling it open and warm to his kisses. "Don't you want to lie in my arms every night in the darkness and be warmed by my body in the chill of dawn?"

"But, marriage..." she protested.

"Say yes, Kit," he murmured.

"Not...not now," she forced herself to say. "Not yet. I need time."

"Okay. I'll give you five seconds."

"No! Time, Matt."

He lifted his head with a sigh, and his hands stilled. He studied her flushed face quietly, his hair mussed, his mouth swollen, his dark eyes intent and warm. "Okay. But until you make up your mind, honey, we're engaged. I'm not throwing myself into that barracuda pack downstairs without protection."

She smiled at the phrasing. "Do you suppose Mother was charging admission?"

"If she was, I want my cut." Matt grinned. "Come on, get up, you seductive little thing, and let me get back to work."

"Who's stopping you?" she teased.

"Well, if you don't mind, I sure as hell don't." And it was then that she realized he'd given her a chance to get out of bed before he did. But it was too late because he was standing by the bed, magnificent in his nudity, smiling at the confused shock in her eyes as she stared at him helplessly.

"This is a first," he murmured. "Remember you said once that you'd been saving yourself for me?"

She nodded, dazed.

"Well, I figured I could save at least one first for you, so I always made love in the dark. I've never let another woman see me like this.''

Her eyes lifted to his. "I'm glad," she said in a stranger's husky voice.

"So am I. Now," he added, winking at her, "get dressed before you drive me to drink again." He turned and started to dress himself as she unwound herself from the tangle of the sheet and got up.

"Again?" She caught on as she reached the door and turned.

He was just snapping his jeans. He grinned at her. "Hal got me drunk last night. I staggered in here half-blind and never noticed the bed was occupied. He did a job on both of us."

"Why, do you suppose?" she asked, puzzled. "Revenge?"

He searched her eyes quietly. "No," he replied after a minute. "I think he was trying to make amends."

"For what?"

"Never mind, honey. We've got some music to face." He let his eyes wander down her body, and he smiled wickedly. "Better wear something terribly unrevealing while we try to explain our way out of this.''

''I've got a great idea,'' she said. ''I found you on a lily pad and kissed you—''

''That's been tried before, and I'll bet the princess's father didn't fall for it any more than the family would.'' He chuckled, reaching in his closet for a clean shirt. ''Move, woman!''

''Yes, Your Grace.'' She curtsied and jerked away just in time to avoid his swinging palm.

When she'd dressed in a becoming wine pantsuit, she found him waiting in the hall for her, and her heart jumped at the sight of him in a brown patterned shirt and tight jeans. He always looked good, but after this morning she felt possessive about him. It would be insane to pretend that he really wanted to marry her, that this engagement was anything more than a ruse to keep the family from being upset about this morning's revelation. But she wanted it to be real. She wanted to marry Matt and have his children. And even though she knew he didn't love her, that he was still involved with Layne, perhaps if they were living together, she could make him love her. She'd work so hard at it!

"Why the frown, baby?" he murmured as she came out of her room.

"Just thinking," she sidestepped, smiling up at him.

He bent and kissed her softly. "Don't think. Just let things happen." He put an arm around her shoulders and led her down the stairs.

All eyes turned toward them when they walked into the dining room.

Matt stared back, cocking his dark head to one side. "Okay, it's like this," he began. "I was sitting on a lily pad, minding my own business, when——"

"Cut that out," Catherine grumbled. "You were the one who told me they'd never fall for it."

"In that case, Kit and I are engaged," he told Betty. "Hal, go break out a bottle of champagne, and we'll start a new breakfast tradition."

"You bet!" Hal chuckled, rising. "Congratulations!"

Betty echoed that, hugging Catherine and

then Matt. "I saw the way you two have been watching each other lately, and I had a feeling this announcement wouldn't be far off."

"Mother, about last night—" Catherine began.

"Now, now, no need to worry about it," Betty said, patting her hand affectionately as she led her to the table. "You're engaged, and these things happen."

There went Catherine's fragile hope that Hal had confessed all. She sighed and smiled at Angel and Mr. Bealy and Jerry and Barrie as she sat down next to Matt at the table and received the mingled congratulations.

"It's been a long, hard, uphill battle," Matt told them as he reached for his coffee cup. "But I won."

"I am not a conquest," Catherine teased, and then remembered how they'd been found this morning, and she turned red.

Matt laughed uproariously. "Liar," he murmured.

"Come down and look at my herd, Matt," Barrie invited. "You and Catherine can cuddle in the back seat."

"You drive an MG Midget," Catherine reminded her. "There is no back seat."

"Well, in that case, Matt, I'll let Jerry drive us in the Oldsmobile."

"Okay," Matt agreed. "Pick us up after church."

Catherine gaped at him. "You're going to church with me?"

"I do go occasionally," he reminded her.

"Once a year."

"So I'll reform," he promised. "After all, a man has to be responsible when he has a family."

"We don't have one."

"We will have." He grinned and stared at her until she dropped her eyes in embarrassment.

Hal came back with champagne, which he opened and poured into delicate champagne glasses, then toasted the happy couple.

After church, which had been a really delicious event—Catherine had been so proud to have Matt beside her and Betty in the family pew—they rode over to see Barrie's new Santa Gertrudis cattle.

Matt stood at the fence beside Catherine, and his eyes widened as he stared. There were six heifers and a bull, and as he studied the bull closely, he burst out laughing.

"He isn't funny," Barrie muttered. "What are you laughing at?"

"My God, are you planning to breed him?" Matt asked.

"Of course, that's why I have six cows. I want lots of calves," Barrie sighed, smiling dreamily, her red curls wafting on the breeze.

"How much did you pay for that bull?"

"Four hundred dollars," she said.

"Didn't it occur to you," he said gently, "that a purebred champion bull that age would bring at least fifty grand?"

Barrie cocked her head, glancing from the bull to Matt. "Is something wrong with him, do you think?"

Matt drew his straw hat low over his eyes. "No, as long as you only want him to pet."

"I don't understand."

"He's a steer," Matt explained.

"Yes, I know," Barrie agreed blankly. "So what's that got to do with breeding him?"

Catherine had to bite her lip. Barrie did love

cattle, but mostly as pictures in magazines. She had a lot to learn about technicalities.

"Barrie," Matt said quietly, "a steer is a bull that's been fixed. Sterilized. Like a gelding horse. You can't breed him. He's hamburger beef, not stud material."

Barrie cleared her throat. She stared at Jerry, who was turning purple trying not to burst out laughing. "You!" she hissed at him. "You knew that! You bought me this super bull, and all the time you knew he was a steer!"

"Not my fault," Jerry choked. "I thought you could look at him and tell."

"I'm so used to looking at beef cattle, I didn't realize," Barrie wailed. "Now what will I do?"

"Well, we can have steaks every night...." Jerry suggested.

Barrie's eyebrows shot up. "Eat Beauregard?"

"Sure, with lots of steak sauce."

"Never!" She bit her lip. "Oh, poor old thing," she murmured. "Poor old bull."

"Don't break your heart over it," Matt told her, smiling. "I know a man who runs purebred Santa Gertrudis. You can get a young

bull for around a thousand and raise him up
the way you want to. Okay?"

"Oh, Matt, that would be lovely!"

"A thousand dollars?" Jerry asked, all
eyes.

"Don't you fuss, either," Barrie challenged. "It's your fault that we bought that
silly bull anyway, and you're not going to eat
him, either. We're going to put him in a pas-
ture and let him grow old gracefully."

"I'll grow old gracefully, trying to pay off
your new bull," Jerry sighed.

"I slave over hot stoves, I break my back
washing clothes and cleaning house..." Barrie
began.

Jerry turned with a sigh and walked away.
She followed him, still raging.

Catherine laughed softly. "Poor Barrie."

"She'll learn," he said. He put a comfortable arm around her and drew her close as he
studied the heifers. "They aren't bad," he
murmured. "Good conformation. Pity she
bought them open though."

"Open?" She stared up at him.

He searched her eyes slowly. "An open
heifer is one that hasn't been bred."

"Oh."

His hand came up to her cheek and traced its softness. "I go hot all over when I think about babies," he whispered. "You've got wide hips, Kit. You wouldn't have a hard time."

Her heart shot up into her throat. "It's too soon to be...to be thinking about that," she said, her voice faltering.

"I think about it all the time," he said, bending to brush a tender kiss against her forehead. "I think about having you in my bed and loving you in the darkness."

"Matt!" Her cheeks burned, and she glanced toward Jerry and Barrie, who were oblivious to them, still arguing.

"They can't hear," he breathed. He lifted his head and searched her eyes intently, unblinking. "Marry me, Kit."

Her legs felt like rubber. It was a terrible chance to take, a risk. But the thought of not marrying him was worse. He only wanted her, but she could change that. Somehow, she'd make him care.

"All right," she said softly.

"No backing out," he warned, his voice deep and low.

"No backing out."

He bent and put his mouth tenderly to hers, warming it, cherishing it. He lifted his dark head. His hand pressed against her cheek, his fingers brushing back a stray wisp of chestnut hair from her mouth. "I'll take care of you all my life," he whispered.

He looked and sounded solemn, and she wondered for one wild, sweet second if he really meant what he said. But suddenly he grinned, and the spell was broken.

"Now that I've overcome your resistance, what kind of ring do you want?" he asked.

She hadn't thought about it. "I don't want a diamond," she said absently.

"Okay. How about an emerald?"

"I've never seen an emerald set as an engagement ring. It would be different, wouldn't it?"

"We could get a band to match," he said. "Diamonds and emeralds in a wide band."

"I love it!"

"We'll go into town first thing tomorrow," he promised.

"But we can't," she moaned. "I have to take the ads to the newspaper."

"We'll drop them off on the way," he soothed. "Stop worrying."

But she couldn't help it, and it wasn't work that worried her. It was Matt. He was marrying her only because he couldn't have her any other way, because the family was so close-knit. But what would it be like when the newness wore off? Would he go back to Layne? She couldn't believe he would; Matt always kept his word. But would he be happy with her? The thought tormented her for the rest of the day, leaving her unusually quiet and reserved.

Chapter Eleven

Matt took her to an exclusive Fort Worth jeweler to buy the emerald. Fortunately they arrived during a remounting, so he was able to buy the flawless clear stone and the mounting and have the emerald set at the same time. Not one of the set emeralds in the store would have done for an engagement ring. There was a diamond and emerald wedding band that matched the stone perfectly, so he bought that, too.

Catherine sighed and sighed over the rings, smiling up at Matt with her eyes full of dreams.

"How about a wedding ring for you?" she

exclaimed when he paid for hers and said it was time to go.

He smiled indulgently. "If you want me to wear one. As long as it goes on my finger, and not through my nose."

"I can see me now, leading you around by your nose," she scoffed.

He ran a lean finger down her pert nose. "Don't you think you could, honey?" he murmured sensuously.

She averted her eyes. No, she didn't. Because somewhere in the background was Layne, and that specter hung over her head like a sword.

"What's wrong?" he asked gently.

"Not a thing," she murmured, and forced herself to smile.

Matt liked a wide gold band, and since her emeralds and diamonds were set in yellow gold, the two rings matched very well.

"Now it's official," he remarked as they drove home. "No more searching looks from the family."

She leaned her head back against the seat. "It's all Hal's fault," she murmured. "If he hadn't lied about it..."

"Never mind," he said pleasantly. "By the time the wedding rolls around, everyone will have forgotten anyway. Do you fancy a short engagement, Kit? I do."

"You just want to get me into bed," she grumbled.

His eyes shot to her face. "Is that what you think?" he asked.

"You haven't made any secret of it, have you?"

He drew his gaze back to the road and lit a cigarette. His brows came together as he smoked it. "No, I suppose not," he said absently. "Maybe I'll have to change tactics again, Kit."

That didn't make sense, but she didn't question it. She gazed at the long horizon instead, and wondered for the hundredth time if she was doing the right thing.

Matt's behavior in the following days didn't make her any more confident. He suddenly became the friendly companion of the days past, and the tempestuous kisses she'd gotten used to disappeared. Now there was nothing more between them than holding hands and a brush

of his lips against her cheek at bedtime. That
worried her most of all, that he didn't seem
interested in her physically anymore. Her mind
was so occupied with the sale that she'd forgotten the conversation they'd had after they'd
bought the rings. Of course, they did talk:
about his plans for the ranch; about her own
need to be doing something besides collecting
dividend checks; about politics and religion
and family. She got to know him on a different
plane. She got to know him as a person as well
as a man, and she loved what she learned. But
would he really be interested in her as a person, if all he wanted was her body? It puzzled
her, more and more.

The newspaper ads were out, the invitations
accepted, and the caterers arrived on schedule
with truckloads of food.

Catherine wrung her hands, shooting worried glances in Matt's direction as the buyers
started arriving.

"Stop turning your hair gray," he chided
during a quiet moment. He tugged playfully
on a lock of her waving short hair. "Everything's going great. You've done a magnificent job."

Her wide eyes searched his. "Do you really think so?"

"I really do." He touched her cheek gently. "After this is over, you and I are going to spend some time together. We have some plans of our own to finalize."

"It's been so hectic," she remarked.

"Yes." He touched his mouth to her forehead. "Want to come down to the auction?"

She shook her head. "I've got too much to do here. See you later."

He winked. "Save me some barbecue. These cattlemen eat the way they spend money."

"Don't you hope," she laughed.

His dark eyes beheld her radiant face. Her green eyes were like dew-kissed grass, her complexion all peaches and cream in its frame of chestnut hair. She was wearing a floral sundress with a halter top and she looked gorgeous.

"I've never seen anything as lovely as you look right now," he said quietly. "Beautiful little Kit, you've done a lot of growing up since you've come home."

She smiled at him. "Aren't you pleased?"

she asked. "I was a thorn in your side for a while there."

He shook his head. "Never a thorn in my side. In my heart, maybe," he said engimatically. "See you, pretty girl." He turned and strode off toward his buyers, dignified and urbane in his expensive light denim suit and his boots and Stetson, towering over the other men. He looked as Western as a spur, and Catherine's eyes adored him. With a sigh, she turned away and got back into organizing the tables.

The sale lasted until well after dark, with the last of the barbecue being divided equally among the lingering out-of-town cattlemen. Catherine felt very proud of the outcome. Matt had sold all his purebreds except for one lone heifer, and he wasn't complaining about that. A Western band played waltzes, and some of the men who'd come with their wives were dancing lazily to the music.

Matt finished off a neat whiskey and smiled down at Catherine. "Feel like dancing?" he asked.

He'd taken off his jacket and unbuttoned his shirt, and he looked as wickedly male as a movie star. Catherine went into his arms without a word, loving the feel of his hard, strong body against her. She slid both her hands around his waist and up his back to let them flatten on his shoulder blades.

"Was it a success?" she asked tiredly.

"Very much a success," he agreed. "Have you seen anything of the family?"

"Mother's around somewhere with Barrie and Jerry. Mother was hostessing while I ate. Hal and Angel were here for a while, but I think they've gone."

"The band will go soon," he murmured. "And I've already said my goodbyes. So suppose," he added under his breath, drawing her closer, "you and I find a nice dark spot and make love until we can't stand it anymore?"

Her body tingled. "Could we?" she whispered.

He went rigid for a minute. "I thought you were tired of all that," he said, lifting his head. "You seemed to have the idea that it was the only thing on my mind."

"We are engaged," she murmured, dropping her eyes. "And you haven't touched me for days...."

Suddenly he caught her hand and led her off, away from the crowd, into the study by way of the patio. He left her standing by the open window, and without turning on a light, he went and locked the door.

"What are you doing?" she asked as he came back to her, stripping off his shirt on the way.

"Striking a blow for male domination," he said under his breath. He caught her to him, and before she realized what he intended, he had stripped the halter of her dress down to the waist and pulled her against his hard, warm chest.

"Matt!" she gasped.

"God, that's good," he breathed. He moved her against him, letting her feel the crisp hair on his chest, rough against her taut breasts. "Lift up."

She slid her arms hesitantly around his neck and went on tiptoe, throbbing with hunger. He half lifted her, so that she was against him, breast to breast, hip to hip, thigh to thigh.

"Now," he whispered, holding her there so that it felt as if an electric current joined them. "Now, we dance."

But it was more like making love. She clung, feeling the roughness of his skin against her own, loving the intimate contact of their bodies. Her breath caught in her throat as she moved lazily to the beat with him, loving the feel of his lean, callused hands against her bare back, the sound of his voice whispering in her ear.

"I love touching you, Kit," he said softly. "I love the way my body throbs when it feels yours this way."

"I never dreamed anything would be so sweet," she confessed, pressing soft kisses against his collarbone, his bare shoulder.

"Do it here, honey," he whispered, shifting so that he could press her face against a hard male nipple.

She looked up at him, questioning.

"Men like it, too," he said, smiling as he coaxed her mouth down to him.

She remembered how he'd done it with his whole mouth, his teeth, his tongue and that was how she did it. He stiffened and caught the back of her head, forcing her closer. She drew him into her mouth, and he groaned roughly and shuddered.

"Matt," she whispered. Her hands adored him as she moved to the other side of his chest and repeated the seductive touch. Her lips learned him slowly, sweetly, from his collarbone to the thick muscles at his narrow waist, and he trembled.

"Oh, can't we lie down?" she whispered achingly, looking up at him with eyes that smoldered.

"If we do, I'll take you," he said unsteadily. "Can't you feel what's happening to me?"

She could, and she delighted in the knowledge that she could rouse him so easily.

"You said you wanted babies," she reminded him in a husky, aching tone.

"I do," he said, his voice rough with passion. "I want you, too. But not like this."

He caught her waist and moved her gently away from him, letting his eyes feast on her bareness. "So pretty," he whispered, touching the hard tops of her breasts with reverent hands, then rubbing them with his thumbs so that she gasped. "Mauve and cream. Kit..."

He bent and opening his mouth on them,

tasted them in a silence that blazed with helpless longing.

"Please," she whispered, eyes closed, body yielded. "Please."

He scooped her up in his arms, looked down at her with dark, frightening passion in his eyes, his face. His arms trembled; his eyes ate her. "It won't be perfect this time," he said in an uneven tone. "I may hurt you."

"I don't care," she moaned, reaching up to find his mouth and tease it with hers. "I want to belong to you all the way."

She shuddered. His mouth opened on hers. "I want it, too," he whispered. "I want to show you how bodies join, lock together like two living puzzles. I want that intimacy with you. Only with you. Kit, Kit, I haven't had a woman in so long...." He moaned against her hungry mouth.

The kiss was endless, and during it he began to move toward the sofa. At first it only registered vaguely, what he'd said about its being so long. But surely he'd had Layne? Her dizzy mind went under in a blaze of fire so hot that her skin felt inflamed by it; her arms trembled as they held him. And somewhere in the distance, someone was calling his name....

He stopped at the sofa, shuddering still. He listened, frowning. "Hal," he bit off.

Her fingers touched his face. "Don't answer him," she whispered urgently, shamelessly. She wanted him so it was almost a pain.

"I have to," he said huskily, "or he might walk in on us."

He put her down gently, his hands reluctant as they left her. With a muffled curse, he lifted his head. "What is it, Hal?" he yelled.

There was a pause. "Mr. Murdock needs to confirm something!"

Matt consigned Mr. Murdock to the fiery reaches, but even as he muttered, he was buttoning his shirt and tucking it back into his slacks. "I'm coming!" he yelled.

Catherine stood helplessly as he turned and looked down at her. He lifted the bodice back into place and fastened it behind her neck.

"I'm sorry," he said gently. "It's just as bad for me as it is for you, maybe worse."

"Want a whiskey?" she asked softly.

He laughed. "You didn't knock me completely off balance—not so far, anyway," he murmured. "I'll survive. But I could use that whiskey."

She turned on the light and fetched him a shot glass full. Handing it to him, she looked up at his tousled dark hair and swollen mouth. She looked as disheveled herself. He took the glass and downed the amber liquid.

"Thanks." He handed it back, loving her with his dark eyes. "One day it will happen," he said then. "One day, I won't be able to draw back. If Hal hadn't called me just now, we'd already be in too deep to stop."

"I know," she whispered, looking up with her regret clear in her eyes. "It was never that bad before."

"It gets worse, honey," he replied. His face was solemn now, serious. "It's now or never, Catherine. We have to get married soon."

She frowned, uncertain. "Matt...what about Layne?" she asked gently.

"Matt!" Hal yelled again.

Matt sighed impatiently. "We'll talk about it later," he said, bending to kiss her, very softly. "Wait up for me."

"I wouldn't dare," she replied, touching his mouth with her fingers.

"Well, you may have a point," he agreed ruefully. "We'll talk tomorrow, then."

She nodded. "Good night."

"Good night, little one." He smiled at her, turned and went out. Catherine stared after him for a long, long time before she could get her legs to take her upstairs.

So now there was no more time. She either married him or ran. She went to sleep wondering which was the more sensible.

Chapter Twelve

The bright sun streamed into the dining room, and Catherine found herself eating breakfast alone. Betty was still sound asleep. Hal and Matt had gone to work. It was curious that Matt hadn't waited for her, she thought, especially after last night. She could feel her cheeks burn at just the memory of how it had been, how close they'd come. And if she'd been stupid enough to let it happen, how would she be feeling now? Matt would have no choice but to marry her. Did he really want that kind of commitment? Or did he just have a hunger for her that was so strong that he wasn't rational anymore?

The more she thought about it, the more worried she became. She got up and paced, hating her inactivity. She'd gotten used to going into the office every morning, but now the sale was over and she'd worked herself out of a job. Dressed in jeans and a yellow tank top, she wandered around the house like a lost soul. Soon it would be autumn, and how much would her life have changed by then?

Should she marry Matt and take a chance? Or should she go on to New York? She was at the point of tossing a coin. So much was at stake. She loved him, now more than ever. She wasn't sure anymore that she had enough willpower to walk away from him. At least he still wanted her. Wasn't that enough to start with?

The sudden opening of the front door startled her. She whirled around in the hall, wide-eyed, to find Matt standing just inside the screen door.

"Good morning," she said hesitantly. She felt shy with him all of a sudden, girlish.

"Good morning," he replied. "Have you eaten?"

"Yes."

He held out his hand. "Come for a ride, Catherine."

She took the outstretched fingers, letting him lock them with hers, and followed him out into the warm sunshine.

"Where are we going?" she asked when he'd put her into the front seat of the Lincoln and climbed in behind the wheel.

"To the Comanche Flats airstrip. From there we fly to the Dallas-Fort Worth airport."

"And from there?" she persisted.

"We aren't going anywhere. We're going to meet somebody there."

"Oh." She felt vaguely disappointed. She liked shooting off into the sky with Matt, but this short hop seemed less than thrilling. She fingered the leather upholstery. "Did you arrange for all those shipments?" she murmured.

"From the sale?" He nodded. He lit a cigarette, glancing at her curiously with his black, black eyes. He took a draw on the cigarette and stared ahead at the long highway. "Catherine, about last night..."

And here it comes, she told herself, stiffening. He was going to apologize for what had happened. Or admit that he'd suddenly realized he couldn't go through with the wedding. Or...

"I didn't sleep much," he continued quietly. "I've been thinking about us. About the way this engagement happened."

"If you want to call it off..." she began hesitantly.

He glanced at her. "Is that what you want, honey?" he asked gently. "What you really want? Have I pushed you into a corner?"

She studied his hard face. Yes, here it is. Her chance to escape. To be free. She gnawed on her lower lip. Why was it so hard to say the words?

"You don't have to say it," he said then. "I think I understand how you feel. I haven't really given you a chance to make up your own mind, to sort out how you feel about me. Catherine, if you'd rather not marry me, I'll let you go—to New York, if that's what you want."

He looked strange this morning. Hard-eyed and stiff and unapproachable. "How do you feel about it?" she asked.

He laughed curtly and took another draw on the cigarette. "We're not discussing me."

"No, we never do," she said abruptly, glaring at him. "I never know how you feel or what you think. You're a stranger half the time."

"How can I be anything else at this point?" he asked glancing at her pointedly. "You're as much a clam as I am."

She started to speak but closed her mouth on a heavy sigh. She didn't know what he wanted, but she had a cold feeling that he'd had second thoughts.

"If I asked you to let me break the engagement?" she probed.

"I would," he replied.

"Gladly, it sounds," she said lightly. "You don't want a noose around your neck anyway, do you?"

He studied her for a long moment, his eyes quiet, haunted, then he turned his gaze to the road. "If New York is what you really want, tell me!" he bit off.

She took a deep breath. "All right. It's what I really want!" she lied.

He didn't say a word for another mile. "Okay," he said then. "We're quits."

Her eyes filled with tears that she was too proud to let him see. It was no good telling herself this was the best way. She was hurting too much. She started to take off the emerald ring, but her fingers wouldn't cooperate. Soon, she promised. Soon I'll do it; I'll give it back.

Sitting beside him in the small private plane as he flew them to the airport, she refused to speak until they'd taxied to a stop and were walking into the terminal.

"Why are we here, anyway?" she asked in a husky tone.

"To meet Layne. She's agreed to meet me here so I can sign some papers."

"Layne!" She glared at him, lips trembling, eyes flashing. "You brought me here, knowing that...that woman is coming?" she demanded. "How could you!"

His eyebrows shot straight up. But before he could say anything, he was being paged to the information desk.

"This way," he said, propelling her with a steely hand. He glanced down at her. "When we're through here, you're going to explain that outburst.''

"Don't hold your breath, big man," she retorted.

He dragged her to the desk, where a tall, heavyset woman with black hair waited, smiling down at a young boy about six years old.

"Hello, Layne," a grinning Matt greeted her, holding out a hand to shake hers. After introducing the two women, he said to Layne, "Thanks for making this rushed trip."

"No problem." Layne laughed. "My youngest wanted to ride with Mama, so I let him come along. I have three, you know," she confided to a thunderstruck Catherine. "My husband and I work all hours just to pay the grocery bills. You should see how much food they can put away!"

Matt smiled, but without much feeling. He signed the necessary papers while Catherine stood stock-still nearby, her heart as cold as November snow. She'd really done it now. She'd lied, telling Matt she didn't want to marry him, only because she was sure he was involved with Layne. And here was Layne, a very married lady who obviously loved her family and whose only interest in Matt was making a sale. Catherine wanted to die. How could she have misread the situation so horribly? And worse, why had Matt deliberately misled her?

She waited until he finished, then said goodbye to Layne and followed Matt back out to the airplane. Stony silence prevailed until after they'd landed at the Comanche Flats airstrip.

"She's married," she said dully after he'd put her in the car and gotten in beside her.

"Yes," he said quietly.

"Angel said she called you all the time."

"Of course. We've been working on this deal for a long time. There were days when I wouldn't even let Angel put her through to me, I was so sick of the wrangling." He lit a cigarette with a hard sigh. "We closed the deal this morning."

"I...Hal said she was your latest," she murmured. "And you let me think she was. Why?"

He shrugged. "It was all part of the game, honey. I thought I was winning, for a while there."

So she'd been right. Layne was fiction, but

the game wasn't. He'd only been amusing himself. Tears stung her eyes as she stared out at the landscape.

They drove back to the ranch in a stark kind of silence, and as she glanced at Matt, she found the stranger there—a cold, unsmiling man who looked as if he'd lost his whole world. Where was the pleasant, teasing, laughing man of weeks past? And then she began to wonder if that hadn't been a mask he'd worn to keep her from seeing the very serious man underneath. She felt as if she'd never really known Matt at all. Now New York was more a terror than an anticipated delight.

He stopped at the front porch and waited for Catherine to get out. And she had a premonition that if she did, it would be the end of everything between them. Outside, clouds had formed overhead and it was just beginning to sprinkle rain. But she felt much more stormy than the weather.

She turned to him, but he wouldn't even look at her. His face was harder than she'd seen it in weeks.

"Matt?" she began softly.

"There's nothing more to say, Catherine," he replied quietly. "It's all over."

"I should have trusted you, shouldn't I?" she asked, as the puzzle pieces began to fall into place. "I should have realized that you aren't the kind of man who'd court one woman and keep another on the side. And I didn't even begin to see it."

His head turned slowly, his eyes solemn and even as he studied her. "Perhaps you didn't want to see it," he remarked, and drew on his cigarette. "You're very young, Catherine. I should have taken that into account. You didn't have the experience to understand what was happening."

She smiled wistfully. "I feel pretty old right now, if you want to know."

He shook his head. "You needed time, and I couldn't give it to you. Patience isn't one of my virtues." He finished the cigarette and put it out. "Go to New York, honey. Get your wanderlust out of your system. Maybe you'll find someone up there's who's closer to your own age—"

"No!"

She hadn't meant to do that, to put quite so

much feeling into that one word. But her voice broke on it, and Matt's head jerked around when he heard her. He searched her anguished face, and his chest was still, as if he'd stopped breathing.

Her eyes locked into his, helpless, hungry. Her lips trembled as she tried to find words and failed.

His face hardened even more; his eyes blazed as they returned her hungry stare. "I love you," he said roughly. "Is that what you want to hear, Kit?"

Tears came down her cheeks like silver rain, and she managed a watery smile. Rainbows. All her dreams coming true at once. Heaven.

"Oh, God. Come here!" he whispered unsteadily and reached for her.

She felt his mouth devouring hers, his arms crushing her against his hard chest. And outside, the rain beat on the metal roof while she got drunk on Matt's warm mouth and slid her hands lovingly into his dark, cool hair.

"Love me," she whispered as his mouth opened and brushed lovingly against hers. "Love me, Matt."

His hands made magic on her body, finding

their way under her blouse to warm, soft curves that he quickly made bare and caressed with aching tenderness. His mouth pressed her head back into his shoulder with its hungry, ardent pressure and he made a rough sound under his breath, a groan.

"I was jealous," she whispered, breathily in his ear as she pressed closer. "I loved you, and there was Layne, and I was so afraid to take you seriously. I couldn't have gone on living if it hadn't been true, if you'd only been playing."

He laughed gruffly and his arms contracted lovingly, pressing her yielded body against his own as the rain made a veil between them and the world. "That was the biggest joke of all," he whispered, "that I was amusing myself with you. My God, I've been out of my mind waiting for you, waiting for you to see me as a man. You came out on the flats and announced you were going to New York, and I felt my world crashing down on my head! And Hal didn't help. I could have shot him for interfering."

"I could have, too," she breathed, nuzzling her face into his throat. "But with all the women you had running after you, I couldn't believe you'd ever wanted me.''

"Window dressing,'' he confessed, lifting his head to pin her with his dark, warm eyes. "Kit, do you remember the night we almost went too far, at the barbecue? And I told you it had been so long since I'd had a woman?''

She nodded, coloring a little with the fierce sweetness of the memory.

He touched her mouth with fingers that had a fine tremor. "I haven't had a woman in two years, Kit,'' he whispered huskily. "Not since the day I opened my eyes and realized that I'd been possessed by soft green eyes and a laughing young face that were all I wanted to see for the rest of my life.''

She didn't know what to say. She touched his face, wondering at the love she could read in it so plainly. "How could I have been so blind?'' she whispered.

"How could I?'' he replied. "All the signs were there, but I was too strung out worrying about losing you to read them. Kit, I tricked you into this engagement, but I wanted it so desperately. I want to marry you. To have children with you. To lie in the darkness with you and love you all the days of my life. If you leave me, I might just as well lie down and die," he murmured fervently against her warm mouth. "I love you...!"

She felt the wetness of her tears in the kiss and lifted her body against him, savoring the newness of belonging, smiling breathlessly as his searching hands went under her shirt and took possession of the soft weight of her breasts.

"Did you know I was in bed with you the night Hal tricked me?" she whispered shakily, then caught her breath as his thumbs edged out and found the evidence of her arousal.

"I knew," he confessed with a faint smile. "But it was too good an opportunity to miss. For once, old Hal did the right thing and tried to make amends, and it didn't backfire. I took shameless advantage of it. I thought if I could get you to marry me, I could teach you to love me."

"And I didn't need teaching," she murmured softly.

"Well, not in that," he agreed. "But in other ways...."

"You'll have to marry me, then," she told

him. "And..." She gasped, lifting herself closer to his searching hands. "Oh, Matt, it had better be soon!"

"I feel the same way," he murmured at her mouth. "I want you so badly, Kit. I want the physical expression of love, the joining, the oneness. I've never had that because, until now, I've never loved."

He made it sound so beautiful, so much a part of loving and being loved. She looked up at him with her heart in her eyes, feeling already that bonding of skin on skin, of voices urgent and hungry, of hands touching, bodies locking together in a rhythm that was already familiar. Her face reddened at the vivid images, and he saw that look and crushed her mouth with his, groaning.

"I can picture it, too," he whispered unsteadily, holding her even closer. "Picture it, feel it, the way you'll be with me. Your body under mine, your voice breaking, your hands clutching at my hips—"

"Matt!" She shuddered with the sweetest kind of pleasure and hid her face against his pounding chest.

"I'll be so damned tender, Kit," he breathed. "I'll cherish you."

"Yes, I know," she whispered, closing her eyes. "I love you so."

"Hush, and kiss me."

By the time he'd had enough, the windows were fogged up all over, closing out the world, and she lay in his arms looking up at him with lazy, seductive eyes.

"I guess you won't let me work?" she teased.

"If you want to," he replied surprisingly. "You can publicize all my sales."

"You'll have to pay me a good salary," she added.

He smiled slowly, looking dark and handsome and wildly possessive. "Oh, I'll do that. And you get great fringe benefits."

"Like insurance and retirement?"

"Plus you'll get to sleep with the boss," he added, grinning from ear to ear.

She peeked up at him through her lashes. "Nice benefits."

"Reciprocal, too," he murmured, letting his eyes run slowly over her body.

He bent to her mouth again, and just as he

started to draw her closer, they heard voices outside the car.

"Are you sure they're in there?" Hal was asking. "Windows sure are foggy."

"That's why I'm sure they're in there," Betty replied. "Go on, knock on the window."

"I don't know. Matt's got a pretty hard right cross."

Smiling at Catherine, Matt sighed, as he reached over and flicked on the ignition. He let the power window down a couple of inches.

"Well?" he asked Hal and Betty, who were standing huddled under an umbrella.

They took in the picture: swollen mouths, dreamy looks, Catherine's crumpled shirt, Matt's shirt half unbuttoned. They grinned.

"How about some champagne?" Hal offered.

"Get it out," Matt agreed. "It feels like a champagne morning, all right."

Catherine looked up into the warmly possessive eyes of her husband-to-be, the laughter soft and loving on her face. Yes, it felt like a champagne morning. And it would, all the mornings of their lives. She told him so as the others disappeared, and she watched him smile slowly as he eased the window back up and bent again to her mouth.

Take 3 of "The Best of the Best™" Novels FREE

Plus get a FREE surprise gift!

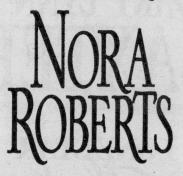

National Bestselling Author

MARY LYNN BAXTER

"Ms. Baxter's writing…strikes every chord within the female spirit."
—Sandra Brown

LONE STAR Heat

SHE is Juliana Reed, a prominent broadcast journalist whose television show is about to be syndicated. Until the murder…

HE is Gates O'Brien, a high-ranking member of the Texas Rangers, determined to forget about his ex-wife. He's onto something bad….

Juliana and Gates are ex-spouses, unwillingly involved in an explosive circle of political corruption, blackmail and murder.

In order to survive, they must overcome the pain of the past…and the very demons that drove them apart.

Available in September 1997 at your favorite retail outlet.